ONE CRUEL NIGHT

ONE CRUEL NIGHT

K.A. LINDE

To Paris,
You're a thief. You stole my heart.
And I never want it back.

CHAPTER 1

*R*ich, decadent, self-indulgent depravity.

That was my first thought when I surveyed the party I was currently crashing.

"What the hell am I doing here?" I asked barely above a whisper.

But my best friend still heard me.

"To loosen you up, Natalie," Amy said. She nudged me forward into the room on the stiletto heels she'd all but forced onto my feet before we left her flat.

"In a dress *this* tight?" I gestured to the skintight black designer dress she'd pulled out of her outrageous closet for me.

Bohemian was a bit more on-brand for me, but I'd relented when I saw how eager she was. We'd been spending all summer in Paris and managed to stay out of trouble. I shouldn't have even been surprised that she'd gone looking for it our last weekend. Trouble was Amy's middle name.

"You look hot. Now, shut up and have a good time." Amy pushed through the packed penthouse party and into the mayhem.

People danced to the music blasting in through unseen speakers. Bodies crushed together, hands touching, hips grinding. It was possible a couple was having sex in a darkened corner. Alcohol flowed like a fountain. Cocaine lay white as snow across a coffee table. For a split second, I saw the Eiffel Tower light up a window before we moved into another room.

"Do you even know where you're going?" I asked, clutching on to Amy's hand.

"The bar, obviously. Then, we'll see if Enzo showed."

I cringed. This was going to be an interesting night.

Amy found the bar with ease and ordered us both vodka tonics. She promptly downed hers and started in on number two before I even had more than a sip of mine. I was more interested in people-watching. It was a writer's curse. Or that was what my dad always called it when I was able to recall useless information about strangers. I had a knack for details and never forgot a face.

That was how I found Enzo long before Amy. We'd met him a total of one time before he slipped Amy the address to this party and told her to crash if she dared. Amy could never resist a dare.

"*Ma belle*," Enzo said in his thick French accent.

I admired him as he approached. His dark brown skin gleamed under the stark white shirt he'd left unbuttoned to the middle of his chest. His black hair coiled alluringly. He had delicate hands with paint still on his fingertips, as if he'd rushed over here while still working on some new masterpiece. I'd seen his work. I knew, one day, he'd be famous.

"Enzo," Amy said, fluttering her eyelashes at him. "We made it."

He kissed Amy on both cheeks in greeting. "So you did. So you did." His eyes cut to me. "Both you and your little friend."

"Natalie," Amy interjected. "She's with me."

He shrugged as if he didn't care one way or another. His eyes were only on Amy. That was normal between the two of us. Amy stood out. I hid behind the page.

"Any trouble with the doorman?" Enzo asked.

He slung an arm around Amy's shoulders and moved them toward another room. I sighed and followed. Typical.

"We're here, aren't we?"

Amy had paid the doorman to let us through. Not that she'd say that. Her parents were rich but not *this* rich.

Enzo seated us in an enormous space that I could only guess was a den. Enzo's friends greeted us. While they were all handsome, they were all definitely Amy's type. She loved artists. And her parents hated them. Win-win in her eyes.

But the line of vapid narcissists all seemed the same to me. I wasn't sure I had a type. If I did, they weren't any of these men. I willingly relinquished center stage to Amy and let my eyes drift out toward the exquisite balcony that wrapped around the full exterior of the room.

To the four sets of open French doors. And the white curtains ruffling in the faint breeze off the Seine. To the intricate crown molding that accented the soft blue walls. The dozen people outside laughing. All gorgeous, confident, and utterly carefree like Amy.

But my eyes were drawn to one man.

Gooseflesh broke out over my skin. I'd seen this mysterious man before. He must be staying at a flat near the one I'd been staying at all summer with Amy because I'd seen him in the park across the street on multiple occasions. He was always scribbling furiously in a notebook or gazing off unseeingly into the distance, as if a profound thought might hit him at any moment. He'd seemed intense...even from afar. Intense and charming.

Now, he was here.

"Amy," I said, gently nudging her.

"Hmm?" Amy asked, prying her eyes away from Enzo for a minute.

"Do you recognize that man?"

Amy followed my line of sight and frowned. "Should I?"

"I've seen him before in the park by our flat."

Amy pursed her lips. "Did you meet Enzo's friend, Alexandre? He's hot, charming, and here right now."

I glanced over at Alexandre and smiled halfheartedly. I didn't know what it was about this other man. Maybe I did have a type, and men who wrote furiously in notebooks was it.

"Yeah, but…do you think…"

"Natalie," Amy said, "no way."

"What? No way what?"

"Absolutely not."

I widened my eyes in confusion. "Why are you freaking out?"

"I know that kind of guy. You should stay far, far away from the likes of him. He has bad news written all over him."

I laughed at Amy. "You haven't even met him."

"I don't have to meet him. I can just tell. Trust me. You do not want to get tangled up with *that*." Amy spread her arms out. "Especially when you have a buffet of hot Parisian artists."

My eyes roamed the gorgeous stranger. What about him would make Amy tell me to run for the hills? He exuded a confidence that had clearly been bred into him. He wore high society like a second skin in a tailored black suit. His dark hair shone in the chandelier lighting, and the candles flickered against his sunkissed skin. He had eyes like a hawk—observant, cunning, and wicked. Lips that were sensual and inviting. A body made to worship. He was exquisite. A work of art.

Amy touched her finger to my chin and forced me to look back at her. "Don't even think about it, Nat."

But I was thinking about it.

I was definitely thinking about it.

"What's the worst that could happen?" I mused.

"Fine. It's your funeral," Amy said. "But just know

that I warned you. I don't want to have to say I told you so, but I will."

"You're so dramatic."

Amy waved her hand at me, telling me to run off and play. Even though she thought it was a horrible idea, she'd let me make my own bad choices.

But I should have taken her advice. I should have known that Amy was only looking out for me. She wouldn't have warned me off of this mysterious stranger for no reason.

When he finally saw me, everything screeched to a halt. Amy's advice fluttered out of my mind like a quick summer breeze. His attention made me feel as if I were trapped in a spider's web. I could struggle to escape, but it would be pointless. The end result would always be the same.

Then, he smiled—a controlled, devious thing—and moved toward me.

I let the web cocoon me and prepared for his imminent arrival.

CHAPTER 2

*I*t was his eyes that slayed me first.

Cerulean water on a cloudless day. A colorless diamond, bright and clear with just as many facets. Brimming with emotion and mischief and pure ego. A thousand novels could be penned from one look in those eyes and never hope to capture them.

"Hi," I blurted out with all the couth of an elephant at a tea party.

The corners of his mouth turned up in something that wasn't quite a smile. But it was certainly an invitation. My heart rattled in its cage, a bird desperate to escape its long-forged prison.

"*Bonsoir*," he said. "You're new here."

"Is it that obvious?"

"No. It's just that I would have remembered you if I'd seen you before."

A blush crept up my neck and settled into my cheeks. "Well, I remember you."

He raised his eyebrows. "We've met before?"

I bit my lip and shook my head. I couldn't believe I'd even said that. It was going to sound creepy that I'd seen him in the park. That I remembered him writing in his notebook. Most people only noticed as much as they needed to fill in the gaps. My brain didn't work like that. Not when it might all end up in my next unfinished manuscript.

"Well, no," I said hesitantly. "I recognized you from the park."

"Is that so?"

"Yes, you're always writing so intently in your notebook," I admitted.

It was the right thing to say. A real smile split his face. "That I am. Now, you leave me at a disadvantage."

"How so?" I asked, nearly breathless as he stepped closer to me.

"You already know that I'm a slave to writing, and I know nothing about you."

I swallowed. I should have felt uncertain about him and his cool charm, but I felt nothing of the sort. Amy's warning felt like days ago, not minutes. And I was completely at ease with him. More than I was with any stranger I'd met previously.

"My name is Natalie," I said, offering him my hand.

"Natalie." He tasted my name like a fine wine.

Then, he took my hand in his, but instead of shaking, he brought it up to his lips and placed a tender kiss on it. Goose bumps erupted on my skin.

"I'm Penn."

I giggled. "Like what you write with."

"Never heard that before," he said with a casual laugh of his own.

He gestured toward the balcony he'd come from, and I walked at his side back to the stunning city view.

"Is Penn...short for something?"

He shook his head. "My parents like unusual names."

"So, just Penn?"

"That's right."

He leaned one elbow back against the railing and slid the other hand into the pocket of his suit pants. I suddenly felt as if I'd slipped right into a James Bond film. Except I was anything but a Bond girl, and things like this didn't happen to me.

Up until this encounter, I would have said that men this attractive didn't exist in the real world. They graced magazine covers, starred in blockbuster movies, and modeled for designer brands. If they existed outside of that glamorous life, then they definitely were not in Charleston. I hadn't seen them in Kansas or Texas or Colorado or any of the other places my dad had ended up throughout his career in the Air Force.

"So, what's your favorite part of Paris so far?" Penn asked. "Other than watching me write in my notebook."

I laughed and eased forward against the balcony. "Probably watching the Eiffel Tower twinkle when the sun sets."

"Ah, yes. A favorite tourist pastime."

I scoffed. "If I'm a tourist, what does that make you? You're American, too."

"I stopped being a tourist a long time ago. But yes, I admit I am American. New York. You?"

"I'm not from anywhere," I told him. When he looked at me in confusion, I clarified, "My dad was in the Air Force. He retired in Charleston."

"Transient and adaptable," he guessed.

"Suppose so."

"What else have you done since being in town?"

I shrugged but saw that he was actually intently staring at me. His body language was completely fixated on me. His eyes slid to my lips and back up as he waited for an answer.

"All the regular stuff—Eiffel Tower, Arc de Triomphe, Notre-Dame, Louvre, Basilica du Sacré-Cœur, the Champs, Versailles. I've been staying all summer with my best friend. She's been here before and showing me the sights."

"Sounds like a good friend."

"What about you?" I asked. "If you're not a tourist, what have you been doing?"

"Trying to get my head on straight."

I arched an eyebrow. "What does that mean?"

"New York is too loud. I needed another point of view. To walk the streets where the greats walked before me and eat at the cafés where they ate and drink at the speakeasies and clubs they frequented." His eyes grew distant at the thought.

I could see that he was in the same place he'd been when he was writing in the park. That writing, whatever he had been writing, spoke to a piece of him. It opened up something within his soul that also opened up within me.

"I know what you mean. Not about New York," I said quickly, "but about needing to get a new point of view. Everything looks and feels and tastes the same at home. Paris is so...alive."

He nodded. "And you've seen so little of it. When do you leave?"

"Tomorrow night," I confessed.

He pushed off of the balcony in apparent alarm. "You're leaving Paris tomorrow, and you're at this party?"

"My friend wanted to come. She likes Parisian artists as much as I love the sights and sounds of the city."

"This is a travesty. You cannot waste your last night in Paris."

I shrugged and turned back to face the city below. "It doesn't feel like a waste."

"Maybe not, but you haven't even lived the city. And you can't live it from up here," he said passionately, "looking down as it passes you by."

He was right. It was strange to agree so easily with someone. As if Penn understood me better than my own best friend...better than I knew myself. That was disorienting, to say the least.

"Maybe."

"Well then, let's go." He stepped away from the railing.

His blue eyes glittered with anticipation. A thrill

shot through my spine at that look directed at me. And then reality crashed in.

"What?" I gasped. "Go where?"

"See Paris." He gestured toward the door. "I'll show you."

I stared back at him in shock and excitement. I wanted to go. That much was obvious. But...I shouldn't go. I wasn't this insane. I couldn't go around the city, alone at night, with a guy I'd just met. It wouldn't be safe.

"I don't even know you."

"So?"

"You could be a serial killer."

He laughed, a soft, guttural thing. "Fair. What do you want to know?"

"I don't know," I muttered. I hadn't expected that question. Not that I'd expected an invitation to wander Paris with him.

"I'm an open book." He spread his arms wide. "Ask me anything."

I scoured my mind, trying to figure out what the hell I could ask him that would make me trust him. Truth be told, I didn't trust easily. Everyone had always said that moving so much in the military meant that you made friends easily. But if anything, it'd made me more introverted. Why try when you'd be out of that school in a year? It was only Amy's persistence and my dad's retirement that had kept me from being a loner in high school.

So, finding a way to trust Penn seemed downright

impossible. Except that...I wanted to go with him. I wanted a magical night in Paris.

"What's your deepest, darkest secret?" I asked on a whim.

His eyes slid sideways to mine, and a clever grin spread on his lips. "You couldn't handle that one."

I raised my eyebrows sharply. "I, uh...what?" I stammered out.

Then, he was laughing. "You should see your face right now."

"Oh my god!" I muttered, smacking him on the arm.

"It was a joke. Just a joke." He put his hand over his heart and tried to control his laughter. "You were too easy a mark."

"Well, that's really convincing."

But his smile eventually won me over, and I was gasping with laughter, too. People were even looking at us, and in that moment, I couldn't care less.

"You really thought I had some terrifying secret."

"You were supposed to reassure me."

He shrugged. For a second, he turned pensive, as if seriously considering the question that I'd posed for him. That far-off look graced his features before he met my gaze. "You really want to know?"

I nodded, slightly breathless as he moved in closer. I could lean forward ever so slightly and brush our bodies together. Feel under the contours of that sharp suit. Graze the strong jawline on my way to those lips. My eyes snapped back up to his, heat pooling into my cheeks.

"I despise my family and all their expectations. Sometimes, I wish that I could live a different life."

Truth.

It was written in every inch of his face and the tension in his stance and the tone of his voice. The man who seemed to have everything wanted a different life.

My chest ached for him. And...for me. For how close that hit to home.

"And you?" he whispered conspiratorially.

"My secret?" I said back just as quietly.

He dipped his chin once in response.

I considered the honesty in his answer. I wanted to give my own truth. But the fact that I really wasn't who I was pretending to be presently wasn't enough. Sure, I was a fish out of water here among the privileged Paris elite. But really I was a nobody from nowhere with parents who hardly had enough to rub two pennies together. And that wasn't a truth I was willing to share. I could give him a truth without the details though.

"I always try to act like I belong, but I never do."

His hand covered mine on the railing. "You belong with me tonight, Natalie."

CHAPTER 3

"*A*my?" I tapped my best friend's shoulder. She was currently lip-locked with Enzo with his hand halfway up her dress.

"Um…Amy?"

Amy came up for air and stared at me with glazed bedroom eyes. "Huh? What's up, Nat?"

"I'm heading out."

"What?" Amy asked, eyes widening. "Are you not having fun? Did things not go well with Mr. Break Your Heart?"

I laughed and admired my crazy friend. "No, things are going great. We're just going to head out together and walk the city."

Amy's mouth popped open. "Um…excuse me?"

"It'll be fine. I turned on that tracker app you use, so you can always find me."

She hopped off of the chaise, disentangling herself from Enzo, who grumbled behind her. "Are you sure about this? You don't even know this guy. He could sell you into sex slavery." Amy leaned in closer. "You'd be valuable, if you know what I mean."

I rolled my eyes. My virginity and the fact that I was still intact was a topic of mutual ridiculousness. "He is not selling me into sex slavery, Amy."

"I've seen *Taken*. I know what happens."

"I will be fine."

"I don't like it." Amy chewed on her bottom lip.

"Look, this guy...he's not like anyone else. He speaks my language."

"English?"

I snorted. "Yes, but I meant, he sees the world like I do. He's different. I don't know how to explain it. But I like him, and it's our last night in the city. I want to make the most of it."

Amy finally nodded. "I get it. You're smitten. Just promise me you'll be safe."

"I will."

She snagged my arm. "I mean...safe." She grabbed her purse off the floor where she'd abandoned it and then tried to pass me a condom.

"Oh my god, Amy, we're not going to have sex," I hissed.

She laughed. "Better safe than sorry."

I cut my eyes to the silver foil wrapper and then snatched it from her hand before stuffing it into my own crossbody bag. It felt monumental to even have that condom on me. As if I had made my mind up even though I was getting way ahead of myself.

"Thanks," I said.

"I love you. Have fun!" Amy nestled back into Enzo's lap.

I left her behind and let my gaze sweep to the door where Penn stood, phone in hand, completely at ease. I couldn't believe that I was about to leave this party with him. This wasn't me at all. Still, I'd be lying if I said I didn't want to go. I was drawn to him. From the first time I'd seen him sitting on that bench, I'd known we were kindred spirits. It sounded insane, but I couldn't deny what was right in front of me.

Penn snapped his gaze up from his phone and found me blatantly staring at him. I swallowed back the wave of desire that crashed over me. He arched an eyebrow. A question waiting for my answer.

Would I stay, or would I go?

I nodded and proceeded forward.

Go. Definitely go.

He held his hand out. "Ready?"

"Yeah. All set." I placed my hand in his. A tingle ran up my arm.

"Good."

He led the way from the room and through the rest of the incredible flat we were leaving behind for the city beyond these walls. We took the elevator to the bottom floor and exited through a set of turquoise double doors. I breathed in the fresh air. Paris smelled heavenly at night, like freshly baked bread and fine wine mixed with a unique, warm, musky smell that I would forever recognize.

Penn hadn't dropped my hand, and he held it the entire way as we navigated the city. The distinct cream buildings lined with wrought iron balustrades that I'd come to love. Brightly colored awnings announced bakeries, cheese shops, cafés, and every manner of fine French cuisine.

"Where are we going?" I asked after we walked three silent blocks.

He just grinned. "It's a surprise."

"I can't believe I'm doing this."

"I can. You seem fearless."

I almost laughed. I had never considered myself fearless. I jumped into things with everything I was. It was another part of being a military brat. Every moment counted, and they all had to be perfect. Kind of a problem honestly. Perfectionism was another curse. But fearless? No way.

"Tonight, I feel fearless," I admitted.

"As you should since you have the run of the city." Penn dashed across the street and stopped us in front of a restaurant with a green awning. "Wait here a minute, will you?"

"Just here?"

"I'll be right back."

I narrowed my eyes in confusion but nodded. I'd decided to come with him, so I would see this through. I just hoped he wasn't doing some kind of drug deal or something equally nefarious.

Please don't make me regret this, I silently pleaded.

He appeared a few minutes later with a brown bag tucked under his arm.

"What's that?"

"That is a surprise. Come on."

My curiosity was piqued.

We walked another two blocks toward the Seine. The river wound lazily around the curve of the Eiffel Tower down to Notre-Dame and beyond. Dinner cruises sailed by, taking in the twilight-lit sights. The moon was full overhead, casting an eerily beautiful glow across the entire city.

Penn stopped a few blocks from the Eiffel Tower with a stellar view of the monument from across the river. He padded across the cobblestone path in front of the water, found an open space, and sank down. I watched as he set down the brown package and dangled his legs over the edge of the riverside. He expectantly looked back at me, and it was that look that jolted me into motion.

I crossed the crowded path, removed my high heels, and sat next to him. Our hips touched in the scant space. My breathing hitched at the first heated contact. I cleared my throat to cover the misstep. "Well, this is unexpected."

The shadows accentuated his high cheekbones, drawing a line down to his lips. I couldn't look away as he said, "What were you expecting?"

"I have no idea, but I like it."

"I thought you might," he said confidently. "And you haven't even seen what's in the bag."

He retrieved the brown bag from his other side and began to pull out its contents. First, he passed me a baguette, baked Camembert, and then a bottle of red wine. "Hope you like red," he said as he removed the cork.

"I do."

Or at least, I'd learned to appreciate it this summer. My parents weren't big drinkers. Between my dad's family's alcohol and addiction problems and my mom's belief in all things New Age, my parents stayed pretty straitlaced.

"Though I will have you know, I have had this meal before since I've been here."

"God, I hope so. But if you haven't had Monsieur Laurent's food, then you haven't truly lived."

He broke off a piece of the bread, dipped it into the gooey cheese that looked like Brie but would be insulted by the comparison, and popped it into his mouth. I followed suit, tasting the intricate flavors on my unrefined palate. It was incredible.

Without glasses for the wine, we just passed the bottle back and forth between us. It was sweet but not too sweet. Fragrant with a hint of cherries. I was pretty sure I'd go my entire life and never have wine that tasted as good as it did tonight.

"So, if you could live another life, what would you choose?" I asked, leaning back on my elbows and aimlessly kicking my feet. "From where I'm sitting, your life seems kind of perfect."

"Ah, not is all how it seems, I assure you." His eyes traveled the length of my long, lean legs from hours of swim practice. "I guess I don't know any other way to live, but I'm open for suggestions."

"Well, what do you despise about your parents?"

"Twenty questions?" he asked right back.

I chewed on my lip and shrugged slightly. "Just trying to get to know you."

"Usually, people start with favorite color and what they want to be when they grow up."

"You make me want to cut right through the small talk," I admitted baldly.

"I know what you mean."

"So...very important question: what do you want to be when you grow up?"

"I feel at a divide in that question."

I laughed. "I thought you said this was an easy question."

"I didn't say that. I said that's what people start with." He brushed a stray strand of blonde hair from my cheek. "My parents want me to work for the family business. But I think I want to be a professor." He blew out a harsh breath. "I'm working toward the degree. I shouldn't have to *think* that's what I want."

"A professor in what?"

"Philosophy."

My mouth popped open in surprise. "You are an enigma, aren't you?"

"That is one way to describe getting a rather useless degree."

"It's not useless if that's what you love," I said with more vehemence than I'd intended.

"Tell that to my parents."

"I know exactly what it's like for others to think that your dreams should stay put," I admitted. "My parents think that an English degree, a career in writing, is

21

pointless. I'm smart. I could become a lawyer or a doctor or something practical in business. If only there were a way to tell them that none of that matters to me."

But it was nearly impossible to do so. They believed it was worse than impractical, a waste of money. My parents wanted me to rise above the poverty line. An English degree might as well be a kiss of death.

"Tell me about it," he said, taking another long sip from the bottle of wine. "That secret I told you? This is the main reason. They don't accept me for who I am and then wonder why I'm always trying to escape."

I could feel this mutual truth radiating between us. In some way, we were both adrift. A leaf blowing in the wind on no set course, just being pushed around. And I wanted more than that. Even if no one else understood my obsession.

"I get it," I finally whispered, sitting up and dangling my feet.

Penn set the wine bottle aside and laced our fingers together. Something passed between us then. A current. A mutual understanding. The start of something new. It was inexplicable and incredible.

My body buzzed with excitement, taking in a truth I hadn't let myself see before. I always blamed the fact that I never really dated on my history. Growing up in a different city every year had put a strain on all my relationships. But the truth of it was, I'd never met anyone who really saw me.

Penn's hand moved to my cheek. His thumb traced the line of my jaw, causing goose bumps to erupt on my skin. Our eyes locked in the short distance. The nearly empty bottle of wine made my brain fuzzy and my body warm and inviting. I stayed perfectly still, taking in this moment. I wanted to write it to memory. Just wanted to relive the electricity vibrating between us. The tension was palpable.

Gasps rang out all around us, but still, we didn't break eye contact. In my periphery vision, I could see the Eiffel Tower lights had begun to twinkle. It was a sight to see for sure. My favorite sight in all of Paris. Until this moment.

As the lights shone in Penn's sapphire gaze, he leaned into me. He slipped his free hand around my waist, tugging me just a bit closer to him. His other hand guided my mouth to his. Then, everything else in the universe disappeared.

His lips were soft and honey sweet. Not exactly tentative at first, but the opening of a dance. He was bowing, waiting for my curtsy and acceptance for the dance to begin...to allow us to reach a crescendo. As soon as I reciprocated the kiss, pushing my hands up into his dark hair and tugging on the short strands, all reticence dissolved.

I opened my mouth to him, and the kiss turned frenzied. As if both of us had been thinking of nothing but getting to this moment. I finally saw my equal, the person who spoke to my soul.

CHAPTER 4

"*O*ur night isn't over yet," Penn said against my swollen lips.

For a split second, I considered that perhaps our night *was* over. What it would be like to be that bold. To channel my inner Amy and tell him that we should just leave and go back to my place. I could do it. My lower half was throbbing from one kiss. One incredible kiss that had made every one before it pale in comparison.

I could only imagine what it would be like to move forward. But I didn't speak out. I wasn't experienced in that regard. And even though I'd taken that condom from Amy...I didn't actually intend on using it.

"What's next?" I finally managed to get out.

He leaned his forehead against mine. "I have an idea. It's a crazy idea."

"I only have one night. Might as well make it memorable."

A Cheshire cat smile crossed his face, quick and devious. "That's what I like to hear."

We finished the wine and trashed our impromptu picnic. Between my buzz and that kiss, I was floating above the clouds. Penn directed me down the cobblestone path. My steps were heavy as I let my fingers trace the stone barrier along the riverside. Silence hung between us, but it wasn't uncomfortable or awkward as it so often was. It held taut between us, the tension from our kiss still achingly present.

The moon swelled so large in the sky. I felt as if I could reach out and touch it. As if it were controlling all of this. The two of us just a tide, swept in and out by the pull of the moon. Destined to crash together over and over again. As if this very moment had been preordained. Fate or destiny or divine intervention.

My mother read tarot cards and looked into crystal balls. She deciphered tea leaves, burned herbs, and recited New Age texts about being one with the universe. I couldn't fathom how many times I'd rolled my eyes at her latest rant. But here tonight, it almost made sense. This cosmic aligning that had brought us to the same place and time. That had set us into motion. I couldn't deny that I had never felt this right before. Maybe it was the wine. Maybe it was the thrill of a Paris night. Or maybe it was just Penn.

My eyes cast a glance to his, bright with a reflection of the moon dancing in their depths. "I think, if I had a new life, I'd live here."

"Paris is a thief," he said thoughtfully. "It steals a piece of your heart every time you come here."

I nodded. That sentiment I understood completely. "I've been to a lot of places. I've lived all over, but I've never felt more at home than where I am right now."

"You'll have to come back then."

Yeah, like that was going to happen. I couldn't fathom a world in which I'd ever have enough money to travel to Europe again. My parents weren't wrong when they said that writing was a long shot. Very few made enough money to live off, and even fewer got to travel to Paris, let alone live there. That would be a miracle.

"Someday," I said wistfully. "I just wish they still had the love locks on the bridge."

"They were an eyesore," he said with a laugh.

"Beautiful in their own way."

"But the bridges look so much nicer now without them."

"Probably. I loved the idea of it. The romantic in me I suppose."

"Apparently, the rest of the world agreed with you. That was why they had to be cut off the bridges en masse."

"So much lost love."

"They just moved their love to a landfill."

I rolled my eyes at him. "So romantic."

"Hey, at least their love is still in Paris." His eyebrows knit together as he thought over that statement. "Erm…maybe."

"I guess they should have carved their love into a tree then."

"Why? So it could be made into paper or tooth-picks?" he joked.

I elbowed him in the ribs. "I was going to say that it would have lasted longer, but you're determined to ruin all my romantic notions."

"Me?" He clapped a hand over his heart in mock horror. The quirk of his lips showed how much he was enjoying needling me. "Well, hang on then."

He darted off into the night, leaving me alone, standing by the nearly empty bridge.

"Hey! Where are you going?"

"I'll be right back!"

"You're going to just leave me alone?" My eyes darted around anxiously. Suddenly seeing the sinister in the shadows and finding the quiet eerie.

"One minute. I swear."

I leaned back against the bridge and crossed my arms, wondering what the hell he was thinking. I was all of five-seven in high heels with blonde hair that looked like a spotlight to possible predators. But my worries were unfounded. He appeared a minute later, as promised, jogging back to my side.

"Anyone accost you that I need to beat up?" he asked with a sly grin.

"I could have gone with you."

"Don't worry. I won't let anything happen to you."

I snorted. "My dad was in the military. I can handle myself," I said with a calm I hadn't felt in his absence.

"Duly noted." His smile was devious enough that I couldn't stop myself from smiling back. "Here."

He opened his hand to reveal a gold lock about the

size of his palm. He'd taken a Sharpie and written in surprisingly good handwriting, *P & N*.

A small gasp escaped my lips. "What? How?"

"Now, we have our own love lock. And I didn't ruin all your romantic notions."

He slid the lock into my hand. It was warm from his touch. My cheeks flushed with pleasure, and a sigh of happiness escaped my lips. It was *way* too soon. Of course, it wasn't *love*. I knew that. This was just a symbol of our night. My one perfect night in Paris.

And though I knew it was entirely unreasonable and irrational to feel like I'd just tumbled over a cliff that I had no sense of ever coming back from, I fell anyway.

And I fell hard.

CHAPTER 5

The Palais Garnier was a stunning piece of architecture at the heart of Paris. Amy and I had hit all the main attractions this summer, but though she had a love for art, she had no joy for opera or ballet. Apparently, her parents had dragged her to one too many performances as a child, and instead of instilling a passion for the performing arts, it had ended up being more like trying to get kids to eat broccoli and killing their taste for it for life.

So, I'd never even seen the palatial building, let alone set foot in it.

But I damn well knew what it was.

As a child, I had been starved for art. My mom used to sing opera before she gave up her career for my dad. Not that she was going to be singing in the Palais Garnier, but she had a voice like a songbird. One winter, when we'd been stationed in San Antonio, we'd gone to see a touring ballet company perform *The*

Nutcracker. For a full year, I'd insisted I was going to be a ballerina—until it was clear that I had two left feet. Or more precisely, a fin and swam like a fish.

But I'd loved the grace and beauty from day one.

And my breath caught when Penn brought me to the Paris opera house. The one place in the city I'd always wanted to go and never had the chance. It was as if the man could read my mind.

"Isn't it closed?" I asked.

"Technically, yes."

He had that smile on again. One so full of mischief that I was certain we were about to get in a world of trouble.

"Okaaay..."

"Trust me." He held his hand out.

I didn't trust him. I hardly knew him. And yet, I reached out and placed my hand in his. Put my world in his palm as an offering.

We walked around to the side of the building where a rotunda jutted from the main building with long windows cut into the stone side. Penn guided me to a door, and to my surprise, we entered a modern-looking restaurant with white tiled floors and bright red chairs.

The maître d' shook Penn's hand vigorously, and they began speaking fluent French, effectively cutting me out of the conversation. I knew enough French to get by, but I'd studied Spanish in high school. Up until this moment, I'd thought I'd get more use out of that than French or Latin.

"Come on," Penn said, pulling me forward.

"What were you talking about?"

"The chef is an old family friend, and Pierre wanted to know if I'd be having private dining tonight."

My jaw hung loose. Oh...of course. That was...normal.

"Are we...having private dining tonight?" I asked uncertainly.

He shook his head. "Better."

Penn meandered us through the restaurant, stepped through a door labeled *Staff Only*, and then out into the darkened interior of the Palais Garnier.

"Are we allowed to be back here?" I whispered. I didn't know why I was whispering, except that it felt like we should.

There was no one else on the inside of the building. It was even quieter than outside, and the only light came from soft recessed lighting.

"Define *allowed*."

I couldn't help it. A giggle escaped my lips. I'd never done anything illegal other than speeding and the occasional underage drinking. My father had been in the military, so his punishment for misbehavior was a more fearsome prospect than getting caught by the cops. But my dad was a million miles away, and Penn seemed to know exactly what he was doing. Suddenly, being inside of a theater house at night seemed like a great adventure.

"You know that *The Phantom of the Opera* was written about this theater?" Penn asked. He confidently walked the halls, as if he was well acquainted with the interior of the building.

"I didn't know that."

"Yeah. It was written by an opera critic who claimed that there was a real phantom." He suggestively raised his eyebrows.

"Write what you know, right?"

"And he did. There's an actual lake underneath the opera house."

"Truly?" I asked in surprise.

"Yes. I've seen it before. More a pond actually. When they were building it, they kept tapping into the Seine, and instead of starting over somewhere else, they made it a man-made lake and built over it."

"Fascinating."

"And a chandelier fell and killed someone around the time the man was a critic."

"Perhaps the author was the phantom," I suggested.

"Or perhaps he was a Nick Carraway, destined to stand on the sidelines to Daisy and Gatsby's tragic love."

"Or maybe he was just an opera critic who let his imagination get away with him," I said with a quick cut of my eyes. "What have you been writing in that note-book of yours? Tragedies, as you seem fascinated with them?"

"They are the best kind of story," he admitted easily.

"Are they? You don't like happy endings?"

"I don't believe in them." Then, he paused as if real-izing what he'd said. "I mean…"

"It's okay. You're not ruining my romantic notions."

His eyes were faraway for a second. "My parents aren't exactly the model of relationships."

"Are they a tragedy?"

"You've no idea."

I lost the thread of the conversation after that. I didn't know what to say to this broken boy. My parents were a strange match, but no one could deny they were a love pairing. Why else would a New Age–obsessed songbird end up with a strong-headed, religious military man?

And, though I knew next to nothing about Penn, I could tell that he was jaded. Something inside of him was a shattered mess. He was putting on a bit of an act for me. Just as I was surely putting on an act for him. I was never this confident or reckless. I didn't *do* spontaneity. I certainly had no experience with men. Let alone men like Penn, who could charm the pants off a snake. If I was trying to be more than I was, it shouldn't surprise me to think that he was, too. I just didn't know exactly what he was hiding. But I wouldn't mind finding out.

The thought startled me. It was the first time I'd considered beyond this night. To the bright light of day.

"Here we are," Penn said, swiftly pulling me away from that thought.

"Where are we exactly?"

He pulled open a door and tilted his head toward it. "Go on in and see."

I tentatively stepped forward. All of my bravado squashed by the uncertainty of what lay ahead. I tiptoed through the darkened interior to the faint glow of light. Then, I nearly gasped with elation when I realized where exactly we stood. With purpose, I burst forward past the curtains and out onto the massive stage.

My jaw dropped as I looked onto the gilded auditorium and the rows and rows of red velvet seats. A chandelier hung, suspended in a dome, over the orchestra seating. Despite the dim lighting, it was a spectacular, unparalleled view.

Penn stepped out behind me with a smile on his face. "What do you think?"

"I have no words," I told him. "How is this even real life?"

"I wonder the same thing every time I'm here."

"How often are you here?"

"When I was younger, we came every year. It didn't take much to get away from my parents, and this became a favorite spot of mine at night."

"I can see why you love it. It's so grand."

I had never seen anything like this before. And here was a man who had been coming here since he was a child. It was clear that we were from different worlds. He might not know it, but I certainly did. Still, tonight, it didn't matter. I could be whoever I wanted tonight. I didn't have to be poor little Natalie Bishop.

Penn stood at my side and held his hand out toward me. "Can I have this dance?"

I laughed. "There's no music."

"We don't need music."

"I'm not any good," I told him before hesitantly placing my hand in his.

"Lucky for you, I am a great partner."

He tugged me tight into him. He held our hands out and grasped my waist, guiding my own hand to his shoulder. My eyes crept up to his, and something bubbled up inside me—fear but excitement.

Who was this man? What universe had he come from?

Then, he led me in a smooth circle around the stage. His movements were effortless, and he guided us so evenly, it was clear that he had been doing this his entire life. We performed our slow waltz in front of an empty audience, yet the energy between us made it feel like it was a packed house.

"I haven't done this since I was a debutant," I admitted.

"You were a debutant?" he asked with surprise in his voice.

I nodded.

I didn't add that it was the most ridiculous thing I had ever done in my life. That Amy's parents had insisted she do it since she was a legacy, and she had refused until they said they would pay my way, too. It had been embarrassing. All of the manners, etiquette, and dance lessons in the world couldn't make me a proper Southern lady.

"I took my best friend to her debut. My four other closest friends pair off . We all got wasted before the event, and I thought all the parents were going to throttle us when we stumbled through the whole party."

"Oh god," I said with a laugh. "Sounds way better than mine."

"It was an interesting night, to say the least." He frowned slightly. His eyes drifted off and then snapped back to me.

Our dancing stilled, and those entrancing liquid-blue eyes captured my attention. They fixated on me as if memorizing this moment, capturing it in his mind. I drifted closer to him, sliding my other arm up to his shoulder. He leaned down, our breaths mingling in the distance.

I wanted to remember the way he looked at me forever. Such reverence and desire on his face. A face like that deserved to be painted and photographed, so it would never be lost to time. But I didn't have those skills; words were the weapons I wielded. And I planned to paint him with flourished pen strokes and deft metaphor.

His hand trailed up my waist, inched toward my shoulder, grazed my neck, and then cupped my cheek. The agonizing closeness of the movements sent a chill down my spine. My body was eager for those lips, and still, I waited. Letting the moment linger as he touched me with a possessiveness that said all I needed to know. He tilted my chin up and dipped to meet my tender lips.

That was the moment a flashlight beam hit our bodies.

CHAPTER 6

"*Hé! Qu'est ce que vous foutez là? Vous n'avez rien à faire ici!*" an angry voice roared.

"Shit," Penn spat. "We have to go."

I didn't need a translation to know that the guy sounded pissed. Penn grabbed my hand and ran the opposite direction of the security guard.

"What did he say?" I asked, dashing after him.

"Basically, *What the fuck are you doing here?*"

"Oh god."

Penn laughed as he continued running. "Hey, where's the fun if there's not a chance of getting caught, right?"

My inner risk aversion shuddered at that thought. And yet, here I was, running from an angry security guard at night in the middle of the Paris opera house. Perhaps Paris had changed me. Or Penn had.

The security guard was running after us. I knew that, if he caught up, we would be in serious trouble.

We had been trespassing in the middle of a freaking palace. That wouldn't go unpunished. I knew that people with money could get away with a lot, but I doubted that we'd both get away with this.

So, we ran.

And I was glad that Penn knew the way in the dark. My heels were a huge detriment. I walked in them all right, but running? It was more of an ungraceful stumble. Not that anyone but me noticed.

I saw the restaurant up ahead of us. The lights were dark on the inside. It had closed. I bit my bottom lip as real fear coursed through me. What if we couldn't get out? What if all the doors were locked? I could *not* get caught in Paris like this. My father would kill me.

Penn reached for the door, and I breathed a sigh of relief when it sprang open with ease.

"Come on. Get in."

I scurried forward in front of him. He pushed the door shut before the security guard saw where we had gone. The staff still seemed to be in the building, finishing up closing duties. We hurried past them and out into the Paris night.

My breathing didn't even out until we were two blocks away from the building. Then suddenly, I couldn't stop laughing. My hands were on my knees, and I was doubled over. Tears welled in my eyes. All of the fear rippled out in laughter at the relief of not getting caught.

"That was insane," I muttered.

Penn was laughing, too. "I've never been caught inside there. Fuck."

"I cannot believe we just ran away from a cop."

He waved his hand. "It's fine. We got away. That's all that matters."

I shook my head in awe. "Well, what else is on the docket for tonight? I don't think anything can top almost getting arrested."

"The night is young," he said, his eyes twinkling in the moonlight. "I think we can find something to top it."

My cheeks flushed at the heat in his words. Every new adventure brought me closer and closer to the point of no return. I knew I was there already. That I had probably been a goner the second I agreed to walk out of that party with him. But, after being in a spot of real danger, I wondered if I should actually end this. And yet, I knew that it was impossible.

I was having fun with him. And he was right; we hadn't been caught.

If I went back to the flat alone, then what? I was certain Amy wasn't there. She probably had forgotten all about me in her lust for Enzo. That wasn't how I wanted to end my last night in Paris. I wanted adventure. I wanted Penn.

Penn held his hand out. "Shall we?"

I nodded and placed my hand in his. He laced our fingers together, an intimacy in the moment that I couldn't exactly place. It was as if those few moments of danger had shifted the momentum of the night. We were bound by what could have been. Not just what was.

The night air was crisp and fresh. We passed a

39

garden in full blossom as we continued our nighttime stroll. Wrought iron poles lit brightly colored flowers and row after row of square-shaped trees. Matching benches had been placed intermittently throughout. It was one of these benches where I had first glimpsed Penn.

"My feet are killing me after running in these heels. I need a break." I pulled him through the trees and onto the stone walkway, directing us toward one of the empty benches.

He took the seat next to me. "I don't know how women walk in those things, let alone run."

"Well, it was kind of a necessity."

"True."

I kicked off my shoes and stretched out the aching arches. I'd been fine up until the running. Not that I normally wore heels, but I was pretty fit from swimming. I should have been able to get through a whole night in these torture devices. If only Amy hadn't insisted that they made my butt look so good.

Penn leaned back on the bench with his feet straight out in front of him. "The parks really make the city. They're so different from what I'm used to. Don't get me wrong. Central Park is home, but well, it closes at night."

"Are we sure this park is even open?" I glanced around, wondering if perhaps we were trespassing.

"They keep most of them open twenty-four/seven during the summer," he reassured me. "No hope of having an angry cop chase us down."

"Again," I added.

He laughed. "Again. Yeah, exactly." His attention turned to focus on me. His eyes traced the line of my face and down, down, down, all the way to my flexed feet. He had this intensity about him. A way of studying me as if I were the only thing in the universe.

I cleared my throat to break the tension brewing between us. "I thought that I'd fallen in love with the city before, but at night, knowing I'm going to have to leave soon, it's magical. I feel like it's a piece of me."

"Just think, if you'd never approached me at that party, we never would have gotten to this moment."

"Well, if I'd never seen you writing in your notebook on a park bench, then I wouldn't have approached you."

"Ah, writing saved the day again." He fondly patted the park bench. "It all started on a park bench in Paris."

My stomach tightened. I loved it.

Both the night and the park bench.

It felt like a fairy tale.

CHAPTER 7

*P*enn brushed a strand of hair out of my face. "Feeling better?"

I nodded and slid back into my heels. "Much. I can survive the rest of the night now."

"Good." He helped me to my feet. "You up for another drink? I know a place nearby."

"I'm in," I said even though I could still feel the buzz from the wine. Lightweight.

We walked a few more blocks and ended up in front of another cream building. A line wrapped out the front door and around the corner. A red overhang said *Candy Room* in white script lettering. Penn bypassed the enormous line and walked straight for what I assumed was the bouncer at the front. I stared back at the line apologetically.

Penn spoke to the bouncer for a few seconds, and then we were whisked inside to a world I'd never even known existed. I'd been to house parties in Charleston.

Amy had even snuck me into a local bar back home. It was the most lenient for underage drinking, and everyone would turn a blind eye as long as no one drove home. And sure, we'd had drinks since being in Paris but mostly artsy bars, which meant low classical music, live paintings, and deep hipster conversation.

Candy Room was nothing like these other places. It was chic, classy, sensual, and inviting. If I had to dream up a club, I couldn't have even come close to the interior of this room. Red velvet blanketed the chairs and booths that lined the perimeter in an imitation of the Paris opera house. The bar mirrored an old-timey candy bar with drinks inspired by classic candies. The bartenders were dressed up as candy stripers. The dance floor was packed with people dancing to the DJ's jams, and three elevated platforms had poles. A bachelorette party was swinging on one, and I was sure a professional was on the other. Everything was chaos and charm and corruption. I had never been more out of my element and more excited by the prospect.

"What's your poison?" Penn spoke into my ear.

"Surprise me," I told him to cover the fact that I had no clue what to order.

He pulled me through the crowd to the bar and ordered us both drinks. He got some dark amber whiskey concoction. My drink was called a strawberry macaron and tasted as if I were biting into the pastry. I groaned at the flavor. If all drinks tasted like this, then maybe I'd drink more. I downed the drink nearly as fast as Amy had earlier that evening.

"This is so good," I said, stumbling forward into him.

"Whoa there," he said. He gripped my hip and held me up. "That thing has, like, six shots in it. Be careful."

I stared at the tiny glass and blinked. There was only a quarter left. "Whoops. It doesn't even taste like alcohol."

"That's how it gets you." His attention was trained on me. "You don't drink often, do you?"

"Almost never," I admitted.

He plucked the rest of the drink from my hand. "You don't need to be drunk to have a good time."

"I think it's a little late for that." I leaned into him and boldly ran my hand down the front of his suit. "We should dance."

"And here I thought, you hated dancing."

"Ballroom dancing," I clarified. I sucked at that, but I had some experience shaking my ass on the dance floor. It was impossible to have Amy as a friend and not know how to shake it.

"By all means, love, lead the way."

I reached for his hand and let the alcohol direct my steps through the pulsing crowd. I meandered until I found what I was looking for—an enormous open-air patio. I'd heard someone mention it on our way in. What better way to dance the night away than under the Parisian night sky?

The music was a sensual electric pop beat that thrummed through my veins. People pressed in on all sides, letting the beats fuel their hips. I swirled my own hips in an alluring fashion and then turned to face

Penn's awaiting body. I grabbed his suit lapels and tugged him closer to me. His hands slid into place on my sides, and I wrapped my arms around his neck. The way we'd been when ballroom dancing was sweet. Tempting but still sweet. This was *way* beyond that.

My gaze snagged on his, and our eyes stayed locked as our hips did all the speaking. His fingers traced down my body, over my hips, and then dug into my skin to pull me closer and closer until there was nothing between us. Just a breath between our lips. A span that felt like an eternity.

We'd shared that one kiss in front of the Eiffel Tower, and now, it felt as if I'd been waiting all night to get back to that moment. To taste him and the sin that he was offering. I was tipsy enough to do it, to lean forward and take what I wanted. And, still, I hesitated.

He must have seen the hesitation on my face. The desire that he elicited so plainly there. Like a window to every thought. He smirked in the most delectable way and then moved forward just an inch closer. His lips barely touched mine. His tongue slipped out to graze my bottom lip. I couldn't control the moan that escaped me. Even over the drone of the music, he heard it.

"Fuck," he groaned.

I nodded. That was exactly how I felt. My whole body was alive at his touch. That one almost kiss had set my nerves alive for what felt like the first time in my life. Was this why Amy was reckless with her heart? It had never felt this good to have someone touch me. I had never wanted it as much as I did now. It felt dangerous…and yet I liked the danger. I liked the unknown. I wanted more of it and more of him, and I didn't want to think about anything else. I just wanted to enjoy myself and this one perfect night.

My thoughts focused on how to get us alone. How to escape the crowd to get those lips on me. How to enjoy my night to the fullest.

"Maybe we could…" I nodded my head at a back hallway.

His eyes swept to where I'd suggested and then widened. "Really?"

"Yeah," I said, though I didn't understand his surprise. It looked like a secluded area where we could make out. And, right now, that was exactly what I wanted.

He shrugged one shoulder. "All right."

I'd seen other people wandering down this hallway, and I'd figured they also wanted some privacy, but I was not prepared for what I found.

"Oh!" I squeaked.

Penn laughed. "What did you think you'd find?"

"I don't know."

But not sex rooms or a mirrored room to share or, god, a fetish room. I'd seen my fair share of porn. I wasn't *completely* innocent just because I'd never had sex. But that didn't mean I'd seen any of it in person.

My face was as red as a rose, and I couldn't stop the embarrassment that coursed through me. Penn thought that this was what I wanted. He'd gone along with it. And yet…I couldn't deny the appeal of this. How turned on I was getting from being in this room.

I swallowed and kept watching for a second longer. Then, my gaze swept back up to Penn's. He was staring down at me with a hungry, amused look on his face.

He stepped forward, pressing my back into the darkened alcove that nearly hid us from the rest of the people having fun. His stubble scratched across my cheek as he leaned in to whisper in my ear, "You like this?"

"I..." I hesitated. "Maybe."

"And I thought, you weren't ready for the real treats from the Candy Room."

I tilted my head back and stared up at him. I didn't want him to think that I wasn't interested in him. I was. I was interested in all of this in a way that I'd never vocalized. That I'd never thought anyone else would be into. It had always felt shameful until Penn's intrigued and satisfied look.

"What if I am?"

"I wish that you had approached me earlier this summer," he said frankly.

A thrill ran through me. "Me too."

His hand tangled in my blonde hair. My breathing was uneven as he leaned closer to me. His movements unhurried but confident. Then, his lips were on mine, and everything short-circuited.

What had been a frenzied kiss earlier that evening turned into something passionate. As if the hours that we had spent together changed everything. Now, it wasn't just a serendipitous, spontaneous kiss with a stranger. It was heated and laced with tension that had been building all night.

His finger skimmed the hem of my dress, and a shiver went down my spine. He was asking permission. I knew that, if I wanted to stop, then this was the moment. This was when I could say no and walk away from all of this. But not a single part of my body wanted that.

Then his hand slipped under my dress. I gasped against his lips, and he moved to kiss his way down my neck. I tilted my head back, and he slid up my sensitive inner thigh to the edge of my panties.

"Oh god," I groaned as he ran a finger down the lace hem.

Lower, lower, lower. Then, over that most sensitive area. Even through the lace of my thong, my entire body jerked at his touch. I was so turned on between him and this room and the club and Paris. Just everything was super-heating my body.

"Can I?" he asked, looping a finger under the fabric and waiting for my answer.

I whimpered in response. He took that to mean yes and pushed my panties aside. Then, he stroked one finger down the center of me. I shivered all over. My head smacked into the wall, and I didn't even care.

A finger slipped up between my folds and inside me.

"Oh!" I gasped.

"You're so wet," he said with pleasure into my ear before adding another finger.

"Ye-yes."

My eyes slid shut as he started moving inside me. In and out and then in again. Pumping into me with the

48

ease of a practiced hand. His thumb moved to stroke my clit, which made me shake all over.

I'd gotten off like this myself but never from a guy. Apparently, I'd never met anyone who knew what they were doing because fuck. Just...fuck.

Everything was building, building, building. My skin was on fire. A million nerve endings on fire all at once. A flush suffused my whole body. And, still, he didn't stop as he worked my body into a frenzy. As he held me against that wall where anyone could just look in and see what he was doing to me. And, somehow, that just turned me on more.

"Oh god. Oh god. Oh god," I moaned as I felt everything coming to a head.

"Come for me," he growled into my ear.

And that was the moment I saw stars. We were inside, and I was seeing the Paris night sky. My walls pulsed hungrily around his fingers. Euphoria rocketed through me. Everything went fuzzy and warm.

"We should leave," Penn said.

"Uh-huh."

"Come home with me."

"I..."

I had no words. I was still coming down from the throes of the best orgasm of my life, and I never even had sex before. What would it be like to give in and just...be with him?

"Natalie," he said, his voice earnest, "will you come to my place?"

In that moment, we were inevitable.

"Yes."

CHAPTER 8

"*W*ine?" Penn asked when we got to his place.

I gulped and then nodded. "Sounds great."

Everything had been well and good when we were back at the club, but now, I was wondering what the hell I was doing here. He lived in the building three down from mine. We'd been this close all summer. And now, I was here. In his flat. Anxiety warred with fear.

Did I tell him?

It wasn't like I paraded around the fact that I was a virgin. It wasn't a prime conversation starter. Amy knew, obviously. But I didn't share the information, and I didn't know how to say it now. It wasn't like I could just come out and be like, *Hey, P.S., I'm a virgin!*

He didn't even know that I was only eighteen and here with Amy the summer after graduation. These were things I normally thought that I'd share with the guy who was my first. And yet, here I was, with an almost stranger who seemed to know my very soul yet didn't know my age or even my last name.

Man, I was psyching myself out.

"Hey," Penn said, offering me a wine glass. "Everything all right?"

I took the glass from him and had a long sip. "A little...nervous, to be honest."

"Don't be nervous," he said with a soft laugh. He offered me his hand and helped me to my feet.

"I just..." I stumbled over the words I wanted to say. To tell him the truth. And yet, they didn't come.

"It's okay. You don't have to say anything." He took my hand. "Just come with me."

He guided me out of the living room, down a hallway, past the elevator service we'd used to reach the top floor, and to a closed door at the end of the hall. He opened the door and turned on a lamp, revealing what was clearly his bedroom. It was decorated in neutral white and blues with a king-size bed taking up much of the space aside from a desk that was littered with papers. His notebook was on top of a pile of books on the nightstand. Otherwise, it was spotless. Unlike the bedroom I had been living in all summer long.

"I love your place." I took another big swallow of wine and then stepped inside.

"Thanks." He set his keys down on the dresser and then slid his suit jacket off. He draped it across the back of the chair. So casual. He wasn't nervous at all. This was his place, and he was utterly in his element.

He clicked a button for a speaker and pulled his

phone out of his pocket to play some music. The soothing voice of Ray LaMontagne eased my nerves.

"'Such a Simple Thing'?" I guessed. "I love this song."

"It's my favorite of his."

He leaned back against the chair at his desk and observed me wandering his space. I straightened my shoulders and stepped around his bed.

"I love 'Shelter.'"

"Also a classic."

"You have good taste in music," I told him. "Is there anything you're not good at?"

He chuckled. "Depends on who you ask."

I laughed softly and kicked my heels off at the foot of the bed. I was glad to finally be out of those things. "Liar."

"I am proficient at a number of things, but I assure you, there are plenty of people who think that I'm not great at anything."

"Like who?" I glanced over at him with an arched eyebrow.

"My father."

"Oh," I whispered. "Well, I'm going to go on record and say that his opinion doesn't matter."

Penn scoffed. "He doesn't agree with that either."

"Well tonight, you're living a different life, remember? You don't have to live under his expectations. You can just be you."

He tilted his head slightly and observed me. It was as if he couldn't quite place me. As if what I'd said really struck a chord with him.

I turned away from that look and continued toward

the nightstand. I plucked his notebook from where it rested and held it aloft. "Ah, the famous notebook."

I flipped open the leather binding and opened it to the first page, but before I even read a word, Penn's hand came down and shut the cover.

"You don't want to look in there."

"Oh," I said in surprise. "Is it your diary?"

"Worse." He took the worn leather notebook out of my hands. "Philosophical ramblings. I'd bore you to tears."

"I doubt that."

"You don't want to hear my ethical diatribes. Trust me," he said, placing the notebook back where I'd gotten it.

A part of me yearned to pick it back up and read *all* of his ethical diatribes. There must be something juicy and interesting in there if he didn't want me to read it. At the same time, I knew that was ridiculous because it wasn't as if I let other people read my work. I was way too embarrassed to put myself out there. All I'd ever wanted to be was a writer, but actually letting people read my work was another matter. The writing was so much easier than the potential criticism. Or as I always considered it...the inevitable criticism. One day, I'd get my words out there, be an author and not just a writer, but I understood why Penn wasn't ready either.

The song shifted, and I nearly swooned when Calum Scott's "You Are the Reason" came on. Damn, he really had good taste in music.

I opened my mouth to say that again when Penn turned to face me. His eyes drifted to my lips and then back up. The space hovered between us. He reached out and took my wine glass from me, removing what had only ever been a perceived barrier between us. He set it down on the nightstand and then stepped in closer to me.

"I'm glad you're here," he told me.

A hand cupped my cheek. Those cerulean eyes staring deep into my own. The amazing night we'd had spread out before me.

What more could I ask for? This was everything I'd wanted my time in Paris to be. If anything, I wished we'd happened sooner. I wished that I didn't have just one last night but instead had the whole summer with him.

He dragged my chin upward and kissed me full on the mouth. A possessive kiss that said I was his now. That this was how things were going to be. And I didn't want to back out. I wanted this, tonight, here with him. Nerves and expectations be damned. His mouth on mine, his fingers in my hair, his body pressed into me. I couldn't turn down what he was offering. I wouldn't even if I wanted to. And I didn't. I wanted him.

My body was on fire, and this moment with him only coaxed the flames.

His lips moved to my cheek, then my ear, and then down my neck. He turned me in place, trailing light kisses across my shoulder. Goose bumps erupted on my skin when he hit one spot, and I couldn't stop the gasp from leaving me.

"Here?" he asked, kissing me again.

"Oh," I panted.

His tongue darted out and caressed my neck. My whole body shuddered. It was a total trigger. Something so romantic and erotic that just set me off.

His fingers deftly slid to the zipper on my dress, and he moved down my back and over my ass. I inhaled sharply at the cold air on my heated skin. But I didn't want him to stop. I was glad that I'd had a glass of wine so that I had the courage to keep going. I wasn't as drunk as I'd been at the club. I wanted to remember this night after all. But a little liquid courage didn't hurt anyone.

I leaned back against him, pressing our bodies together. Then, he slipped the sleeves of my dress off of my shoulders. It eased down my body, over my breasts, and then my hips before pooling at my feet, leaving me in nothing but my black strapless bra and matching lace thong.

"Fuck," he muttered. "The things I want to do to your body."

He ran his hands down my bare skin. My heart rate accelerated with every touch. He kissed that spot again, and I shivered.

"Wha-what do you want to do?"

He popped the hook and eye on my bra, and it fell to the ground, my breasts hanging pert and exposed.

"This."

He caressed my breasts, gently kneading them until I felt wetness pooling in my panties. He pinched one nipple before bringing the other up to his mouth.

"Oh my god," I breathed.

"And this," he said, tugging the comforter down and pressing me back into the bed.

He ran his mouth down my stomach until he reached the lace of my thong. Biting into the material, he pulled my panties off and hoisted my legs up onto his shoulders. My cheeks flamed at the positioning as he kissed his way up my inner thighs.

I sat up as embarrassment coursed through me. I'd had guys go down on me before, but it had always been an afterthought. Something to do after I gave a blow job. And Penn had already given me an incredible orgasm. I should probably reciprocate that before we got any further.

"Penn, maybe I should..." I sat up, trying to stop him from continuing.

He eased me back into a lying position. "No one's ever complained about multiple orgasms."

And really, I couldn't argue with that.

A kiss on my knee. My thigh. Up, up, up. Traveling north. My legs quivered in anticipation. My core throbbed with each kiss, with every inch he moved closer to the exact spot I wanted him.

He licked once, tasting, testing. I thought I was going to come already. Just that one easy movement had me aching to release.

"This is what I want," he told me. Our eyes met between the V of my legs. "I want to eat your pussy until the only taste on my lips is you."

My jaw dropped, and my whole body flushed. No one had *ever* talked to me like that. It wasn't like high school guys were in it for more than theirs. Penn was different. He was older, more mature. A man.

Then, he did exactly what he'd said he was going to do. He licked and sucked and lapped at me until I was shaking nonstop. He inserted a finger and then another, owning my body and curling up inside me.

Noises escaped me that I hadn't known it was possible for me to make. Little animals mewls and gasping, "Yes, yes, yes!" that felt like it shook the rooftops.

My orgasm hit me afresh. Clamping down on his fingers, practically holding him in place. His soft laugh registered through the buzzing in my ears. It was clear that he also was enjoying the high that I was riding. Enjoying it immensely. Enjoying it so much that I was going to need to do something about it.

CHAPTER 9

*H*is erection jutted hard against his suit pants, and with ease, he popped the button and slid the zipper. His pants were a puddle on the floor. Now, he was just in boxer briefs, and then those were gone, too. My eyes bulged slightly when I got a good look at him. He was...he was...wow, well endowed. Maybe this was the real reason for all the warm-up. Not that I was complaining. Not in the least.

For a second, I recognized that the song had changed. "Lay Me Down" by Sam Smith replaced whatever had come before it, and I knew that I'd never hear the song the same after this.

He popped open the drawer of the nightstand and produced a condom.

"I...I have one," I offered. It felt like the right thing to do.

"Next time," he said with a grin that melted me back into the sheets.

He slipped the condom on and then crawled forward until he was hovering over me. My body tensed, waiting and wondering. My nerves, which had shattered under his tongue, were back. But he just pressed my hair back and brought his lips down onto mine.

"See how good you taste?" he asked.

I laughed. "You like how I taste?"

"I could eat you all day."

I felt the first touch of him against my opening and gasped. He wasn't even inside me, and already, he felt good.

Oh dear god!

"I love all the noises you make," he said, kissing his way back down my neck. Then, his dick ran up and down between my slick folds. My eyes slammed closed. "So vocal."

"Am-am I?" I squirmed under him in response, wanting him inside me so desperately. Maybe I should want to wait, but here in this moment, I wanted nothing more than him.

"I want to hear you scream," he breathed in my ear.

His dick pressed forward inside me. Just the tip. Easing his way in slow and steady. Taking his time to savor me. I had to bite my lip to keep from crying out already. Between his movements, the throbbing in my pussy, and the dirty talk in my ear, I was a wanton woman, ready for whatever he was going to give me.

"Fuck," he growled. "Oh fuck, Nat."

"Yes," I said.

I pushed my body upward, trying to get more of

him inside me, but he grasped my hip in his hand and held me down. I tightened around him hard and tried to shift for more. Tried to ease the ache building inside me. He pulled back and then pushed just the tip in again.

"You're so tight. So fucking tight. Shit."

"Please," I heard myself beg. "Please, Penn."

I'd lost all semblance of self-control.

He reached out and grabbed my arm, holding it tight over my head. Control was completely given over to him, and I didn't even want it back.

He kissed the tip of my nose. "Open your eyes."

They slowly fluttered open to meet his big blue eyes. Then, as he stared deep into my eyes, he thrust forward into me. I might have been tight, but I was soaking wet from two orgasms, and he met little resistance from me. Just pushed forward until he was balls deep inside me.

He rested his forehead forward onto my shoulder. "Forget Aristotle and Plato, this is all the philosophy I need."

My hand tightened around his, and my knees came up to his sides as I felt the full pressure of him buried deep. Then, he lifted his chin, captured my lips once more, and started moving.

Everything faded into the background. There was just me and Penn. The quick yet unhurried movements as our bodies slapped together over and over again. The heated gazes that spoke volumes. The warmth that was suffusing my entire body unlike anything I'd ever experienced in my life. This was a first for me, and I was almost fucking certain nothing else would ever compare. I had no frame of reference, but it felt impossible to consider anyone else would worship me like him.

He sat up and hitched one of my legs over his shoulder. Then, he started the rhythm even faster. My eyes bulged at the depth he reached each time he bottomed out inside me.

"So deep," I groaned. "Oh my god! Oh god!"

"Too deep?" he asked with a conspiratorial smirk.

"No."

"Should I slow down?" He proceeded to ease out of me so dangerously slow that I thought I'd combust, and then he went back in one millimeter at a time.

"Dear god, no, don't stop," I begged.

"Faster, love? Is that what you want?"

I whimpered.

"Rougher?"

I clenched all around him. I couldn't believe I was even holding on. I was right on the edge. Everything felt like it was going to collapse at any second.

"Please." He must have seen where I was because he smiled. "Please."

He obliged. He finished his slow pull out, and then he thrust hard, fast, and deep into me. I cried out. And he did it again and again and again. Until those screams he'd requested burst from my mouth, and I exploded.

Spots filled my vision. I hit the ceiling and floated back down to earth on cloud nine. Everything felt like I was swimming. Barely in my body as I hovered over it all. And I didn't really want to come back to reality.

I wanted to stay in this moment of satisfaction forever.

Penn thrust twice more inside me, and then I felt him finish along with me. He grunted his own euphoria as he came deep inside me. He collapsed forward over me. The force of his orgasm knocking him over. Then, when he finally finished, we both lay, panting from exertion. Sweat lined our bodies, and it didn't even matter.

I reached out and gently ran my fingers through his dark hair. I felt like I'd just run a marathon and could probably sleep for the next twenty-four hours. He nearly purred at my touch. He clearly liked getting his hair played with.

He kissed my shoulder once and then withdrew. I gasped at the absence of him. How I'd felt so full, and now, I felt so bereft. It was definitely too soon for more. I already felt sore, but damn, maybe it would be worth it.

He removed the condom and strode into the bathroom to clean up. I followed suit when he was finished. Then, I came back into his room and sprawled out next to him. He didn't say anything as he lay against my stomach.

"I can still feel your body pulsing," he said.

I blushed. Despite all we'd done, talking about it, when we weren't in the heat of it, embarrassed me.

"That would be because of you."

He kissed my stomach. "You're welcome."

I laughed. "Cocky much?"

"Confident," he corrected.

I slid my fingers through his hair again. "I wish we'd met earlier this summer."

"Don't leave then."

"What?" I asked in surprise.

"School doesn't start until after Labor Day. I'm here until then. You could stay with me."

Fuck did I want that. But I couldn't imagine, in any universe, anyone in my life being okay with that. My parents would pitch a fit. Amy would drag my ass onto that plane tomorrow. I wanted to stay, but I knew I couldn't...I didn't want to break the fairy tale.

"Maybe I will."

"We'll figure it out tomorrow," he said, kissing me again. "We have something else to do tonight."

"Oh, yeah? We didn't see enough of Paris already?"

He slid back up my body, kissing every inch of me as he made his way to my lips. Then, he flipped me over so that I was on top of him. His erection jutted up between us. My body already pulsed at its nearness again.

"I was thinking, round two," he said. His hand slid between my thighs and caressed my clit. "You on top this time."

CHAPTER 10

PENN

"**F**uck, I need a shower," I grumbled.

I slid out of my bed and stared down at the naked blonde from last night. What an excellent choice. Who knew that Harmony's horrid party was going to work out so well for me?

I tossed a sheet over her. We probably should have showered the sex off of us last night. But she had literally passed out after round three. And I wasn't going to wake her up after that. Shower could wait until the morning.

I blearily checked my phone. Six o'clock in the fucking morning.

Jesus Christ! Couldn't I sleep in *anywhere*?

We'd been up until the wee hours of the morning. It would have only been fair to get to sleep in until at least ten. Noon would have been even better. But no.

I flung irritable curse words at nothing and moved

into the adjoining bathroom. The smell of sex clung to everything in my room and on me. It was probably pointless to wash it all off, considering I had every intention of waking her up with my head between her legs and then flipping her over on her stomach and taking her from behind. But I should probably be a little more generous with her than my fucking brain was with me and let her sleep in.

The water was near boiling, and steam billowed from the glass shower as I stepped inside. I let the jets beat down on me before scrubbing last night's escapades off of my body and shampooing my hair.

My skin was red from the intense heat when I stepped out of the shower. I dried off my hair and then slung the towel low around my narrow hips. After brushing my teeth, I went in search of a cup of coffee. It was too early for the housekeeper to be here. So, I knew I'd have to make my own. Better coffee than no coffee in my book.

I set up a French press and left it to steep while I decided how long I would have to wait before waking Natalie up.

A good, long fucking in the morning was almost a better way to wake up than coffee.

Maybe I'd just write while she slept.

Lord fucking knew that I had way too much to get on paper. I'd come to Paris to try to silence all the shit I had been dealing with in New York. I loved my friends —the crew—but they didn't get why I was pursuing a PhD. They wanted to party and have sex every night.

My eyes slid back to the bedroom. Well, maybe I did, too. But I still had work to do. An entire philosophy dissertation that I had to write that would change the world of ethics as we knew it.

I rolled my eyes at myself. Narcissistic much?

I hadn't proven to anyone yet that I was a better producer of philosophy than I was a consumer. And, until I got to that point, no one would take me seriously.

Especially not as a Kensington.

My mood soured at my name. That stupid fucking name that got me in wherever I wanted and left me a trust fund in the nine- to ten-digit range. The name that made people get out of my way. The name that made people wonder why in the hell I was getting a *philosophy* degree when I could be working with my father. The abusive bastard.

The name I had purposely not told Natalie last night.

I'd told her I wanted to be someone else, and she'd let me. It was a privilege I wasn't usually afforded. Never in New York or at Harvard where all of the vultures circled me, hoping, one day, they'd be the one to take me off the market.

No matter that I wasn't even twenty-five, had no intention of taking over my father's business, and had sworn off marriage long ago. If it was anything like my parents' arrangement, then count me out.

Natalie was oblivious to me wandering around as I changed into chinos and a button-up that I rolled to my elbows. I snagged my phone and notebook from the nightstand and went back to my precious coffee.

I opened my notebook to the latest blank page and started in on my night with Natalie. I considered the title and then wrote, *It All Started on a Park Bench in Paris*.

My phone buzzed, and I checked to see who the hell was calling me this early. My mother. Just what I fucking needed. Why the hell was she calling me anyway? It was nearly midnight in New York. She was a state senator in the New York State Assembly. She worked even more obscure hours than I did and cared even less about what I thought about her. She was a ballbuster and notoriously impossible to work for. Try having her as a mother.

I let it go to voice mail, but when it immediately started ringing again, I sighed and picked up. "Hello?"

My mother was crying.

My mother was crying.

My *mother*…was…crying.

I couldn't fathom the fact that Leslie Kensington was actually in tears. On the phone. With me.

Then, I heard the words she had been blubbering into the phone.

I froze.

The blood drained from my body.

I couldn't process everything else she was saying.

I just stood there.

In disbelief.

"I'm coming home," I said and mechanically hung up.

I was in shock.

Then, I didn't think. I just acted. I took my note-book, phone, and MacBook. I slid my feet into shoes and then was out the door and in a cab to the airport before I could even stop to process the fact that I hadn't woken Natalie up.

CHAPTER 11

*L*ight streamed in from white-curtained windows. The sun was shining, birds were chirping…or were those cars driving by below? I blinked rapidly, trying to wake up, and a huge yawn escaped me.

"What time is it?" I murmured into the empty space.

Then, my eyes adjusted.

Blue comforter.

King-size bed.

Clean bedroom.

I bolted upright and stared around the room. "Oh god," I hissed.

Last night came back to me in a rush. Meeting Penn at the party, wandering the city with him, the club, his bed.

Oh god, his bed.

I was still in his bed.

And he was *not* in his bed.

The things we had *done* in his bed.

I shook my head to try to dispel the series of images that floated to the surface. His hands gripping my hips, his tongue on my clit, my hands running through his hair, the yells for more, him giving me more, more, more. I closed my eyes. Had that really been me?

Who even knew that I was that much of a sexual animal?

It wasn't like I hadn't been interested in having sex before this. I'd always wanted to, but despite dating several people, I'd never felt attracted or into anyone enough to go through with it. But last night...I'd been *eager*. Not just eager, I'd asked and had seconds...and thirds.

And now, he wasn't in his room. Of course, there was probably a perfectly normal explanation for that. Maybe he was writing in his notebook, which was missing from the nightstand. Maybe he'd gotten up before me and decided not to wake me. Lots of reasons.

Still, my stomach turned as the what-ifs piled up in my mind.

With confidence I didn't feel, I threw the sheet off my very naked body and went in search of my clothes. My thong was crumpled on the floor where Penn had bitten it off last night. I pulled it back on, my cheeks flaming at the memory. My dress was discarded near his desk. I had no recollection of how it had gotten there. The last thing I remembered was him sliding it off my shoulders. Last night was a wonderful, glorious blur.

And, now, the blur was a dull ache in my very, very sore vagina. Holy Jesus, no one had ever mentioned how much it would hurt the next day after getting ridden into next Tuesday. Or maybe...none of my friends had ever had this problem. And by friends, I mostly meant Amy.

Shit, Amy.

I hastily pulled my dress back on and then located my purse, which was on top of a stack of papers on his desk. No idea how that had gotten there either. I reached inside and removed my phone, which had roughly a million text messages. And the time...noon.

Fuck! How had I slept until noon? I never slept in. I had my dad's internal alarm clock from years in the military.

We were leaving the city today, and I still needed to pack. God, she was going to kill me.

I quickly jotted out a text that I wasn't dead and would be back soon.

To which I had an immediate response that said, *Tell me everything*, and a GIF of a girl wagging her eyebrows up and down.

I giggled and then pocketed the phone again.

Now, the problem of Penn. Did I just stroll out there? Did I say anything? Were we supposed to get breakfast?

My inexperience was glaringly obvious in this scenario. I'd seen enough romcoms to know what to expect, but at the same time, I had no idea.

I couldn't stay in here all day and wait for him to come find me. I needed to make my move. Maybe get his number and meet up with him again in New York. I wanted to kick myself. When would I be in New York? He didn't know yet that I had no money. That I hadn't even had an invite to that party and that Amy and I had totally crashed it. I was a nobody. And his family owned this insane flat in Paris that he'd been coming to since he was a kid. He'd taken backstage tours of the Paris opera house, and the chef was a family friend. Last night had been magical, but in the fresh light of day, we felt worlds apart.

I took a steadying breath. I could do this. Maybe our backgrounds wouldn't even matter. Or maybe I could just say that I'd had the most amazing first time and then leave. Just throw that one out there.

Ugh! I wanted to scream with indecision. Where had all my confidence from last night gone? It was as if I'd lost it all in my sleep.

No, I could do this. Penn felt natural. We got each other on a base level. We could make this work, and even if we couldn't, then I didn't need to be shy around him. Lord knew I hadn't been last night.

I nodded my head once, picked up my heels from the foot of the bed, and then strode from the room. I walked down the long hallway I remembered from the night before and into the living room. The empty living room.

I furrowed my brows.

"Penn?" I called softly as I padded through his flat.

I found the kitchen, which was also empty. A French press was the only thing out of place in the massive room. I turned around and headed back toward the living room. There were clearly a dozen rooms that Penn could be in. Maybe he had a library or an office? Maybe a balcony that he worked on?

I had no idea. But I couldn't stop the unease that hit me. The sick feeling that snaked through my veins.

Maybe he was just gone.

I swallowed back the rising panic and started back down the hallway to try to figure out what the hell was happening. When I turned the corner, I nearly ran smack dab into a woman in a black dress and white apron.

"Oh my god," I said, nearly jumping out of my skin. "I'm so sorry. I didn't know anyone else was staying here."

The woman was a French beauty—tall, lithe, and polished. She spoke to me in swift French. I didn't catch a word of it.

"I'm sorry. *Pardon*," I said, holding out my hands, placating. "I don't speak French." I repeated it again in the jointed French I used to get by in the city, "*Je ne parle pas Français. Parlez-vous Anglais?*"

The maid dramatically turned her nose up. "So, he found an American one."

"An American...what?" I asked in embarrassment.

She gestured to me as if it were obvious, which only made it worse.

"I see," I said softly. "Is Penn still here?"

"He left."

"For the morning?" I asked, my voice getting smaller and smaller.

"What do I look like, his secretary?" the woman

asked dismissively. "I'm a housekeeper. I take out the trash." She looked at me pointedly.

I felt about an inch tall. Maybe less than that. Her disapproving stare only made it all worse.

I'd misjudged him. Oh dear god, how I had misjudged him.

I felt light-headed. I was definitely going to be sick. Or faint. Yes, maybe fainting was in order. I didn't care how dramatic that made me, but everything was crashing down around me. I wasn't sure I could bear the walk of shame back to my flat. Or facing Amy. Oh god…that conversation.

"I'll just…" I gestured toward the elevator.

"*Au revoir,*" the woman said. She lifted her chin and strutted her tiny hips straight toward the kitchen.

I jammed my finger on the button to take me downstairs. I was a fool. An utter and complete fool. Penn had played me like a fiddle…and hadn't even had the decency to send me away on his own.

Young, naive, and stupid.

What a way to lose my virginity.

CHAPTER 12

Down Penn's elevator, three buildings over, and up another elevator was the distance between our two places, and it felt like miles. I wasn't sure if anyone noticed me, the girl struck dumb, as I stumbled around in last night's clothes. France wasn't prudish like America, but still, I was sure I was a sight.

Amy came running out of her bedroom as soon as she heard me enter the apartment. "Oh my gawd!" she squealed. "You were gone all night. All night! I know what that means. Did it happen? Huh? Did it?"

"Yep," I said, gritting my teeth. "It happened."

"Oh no, honey, was it…bad?"

I laughed a slightly hysterical thing. "Bad? No. No, it wasn't bad at all."

"Okay, I'm hearing your words, but you seem to be saying something else. What happened?"

She followed me back to my room where I stripped out of last night's clothes and pulled on a pair of sweats and a T-shirt. Comfort clothes. I handed Amy back her dress and heels. Thank god, they weren't mine, or I might have burned them.

"Uh, thanks," she said. "Now, spill the details. What's wrong?"

"I think we need icing for this."

"Oh fuck," Amy said. "That bad?"

I nodded, and Amy disappeared to go find a container of icing in the kitchen. It was her mother's defense mechanism. Every time something went wrong at work or with Amy's dad or with Amy's grandparents, we would come home and find her mom sitting in the middle of the living room with her hair in a messy bun and a half-empty container of icing in her hand. Icing was now a go-to for trauma.

Amy came back with a container of icing and two spoons. "Here you go, sister. Spill the deets." We plopped down on the bed and dug in.

I took a heaping portion of chocolate icing and devoured it. Sugar hit my system like a two-by-four. "He left."

"Be more specific."

"We had the most amazing night. Dinner on the Seine in front of the Eiffel Tower, sneaking around the Paris opera house, dancing all night in a club. Then, we went to his place and did..." My eyes cut to hers. "You know."

"Yes. That is the part I'm interested in," she said with a laugh, taking her own bite of the frosting.

I held up three fingers, and Amy nearly choked on her icing.

"Three *times?*" she gasped.

"Yep."

"How are you walking? I was so sore after my first time that I pretended to be sick the next day, so I wouldn't have to walk around like a camel."

I snorted in disdain. "No idea. Everything hurts."

"But not just your body."

I shook my head and stared blankly out the open window. "I woke up, and he was gone. He had a maid tell me to leave. She said she took out the trash."

Amy hissed between her teeth. "He didn't!"

"Yeah. So, you were right. Go ahead. Tell me you told me so."

"I don't want to," Amy said. She pulled me forward into a tight hug. "I hate that this happened. I don't want to be right this time."

"You knew from the start what kind of guy Penn was. And I just dismissed everything you'd said. I have next to no experience with men and certainly not with someone like him. And he just played me."

"You don't know that."

I shot her an exasperated look. "I do know that. I thought we were connected on some other level." I rolled my eyes at myself. "What a crock of shit. He was acting the whole time."

"Do you really think he needed to act with you to get in your pants?" Amy arched her eyebrows and held her hands up. "I'm not saying he didn't, just that I don't know that he needed to work that hard."

"He didn't," I agreed. "But I just don't think he wanted to be at that party. All our conversations are just…well, I see them in a whole new light." I laughed bitterly at myself. "He told me that he didn't believe in happily ever afters. That he preferred tragedies and didn't agree with my romantic notions. It was all in front of me."

"There was no way for you to know what he was going to do."

I scoffed. "Except the fact that you told me."

"What he did was *elaborate*," Amy said. "I didn't know he was going to do all that."

"Great. So, I found the one guy I wanted to give my virginity to, who happened to be a total con artist. Look at Natalie, great choice in men." I ate another huge dollop of icing.

"Maybe he just…had somewhere to be?"

I glared at her.

"Okay," she said. "Maybe he's just a dick who took advantage of you, and we can burn him in effigy."

"And now, I'm turning into my mother."

Amy laughed. "That'll be the day."

I flopped back on the bed and sighed. "Did you at least have a good time with Enzo?"

"Truthfully?" Amy asked. "He drank *way* too much and had whiskey dick."

I snort-laughed. "You're joking?"

"Nope. Couldn't get it up at all."

"Oh my god!"

"So, at least you got three orgasms in before Dick-face left. That's three more than me."

I held up my hand. "Five."

"Five?" Amy asked in disbelief. "You're not human. What the fuck?"

"Dickface he definitely is, but the man sure knows what he's doing," I said wistfully.

"Ugh, I both hate and love that this was your first time. It was so good, and he totally ruined it."

"Tell me about it."

"Well, forget about him," Amy said, pulling me back into a sitting position. "We're going back home today. We'll be going off to college in a few short weeks. So, it's like you got it out of the way. Now, you can have as much fraternity dick as you want and not feel like you wasted your first time on some idiot."

I arched an eyebrow. "That's your argument?"

"Oh, whatever! College is going to be so much fun. We'll be roommates. We'll have as much sex as we want. And we'll forget all about Dickface. What do you say?"

I laughed. "Let's do it."

"Good! We should probably pack. We have a transatlantic flight in a few hours."

"Don't remind me," I said, eating more icing.

"You'll be fine." Amy patted my hair and then smiled at me more seriously. "You really will be fine. You know that, right?"

"Yeah, I do. I just feel so stupid. Like I should have seen the game he was playing with me. Instead, I only saw what I wanted to see."

"We all do that when a hot guy blinds us."

"Thanks for being here for me, Amy."

"Let me know if you need me." She smiled and then darted across the hall to her room.

Amy was right. I'd been blinded by Penn. By his James Bond good looks and the way he talked about writing and books. It felt like we had so much in common. But how much of that was real, and how much of it was him leaning into what we'd talked about? Did I make up our connection? Because I'd certainly felt it in bed.

Apparently, I could have a mind-blowing connection with someone during sex, and everything else could be a lie.

I set the icing aside. That was my takeaway. I wasn't going to be this stupid again. If I was going to have a one-night stand, then I wanted to know where I stood in that regard. Because I didn't want to fool my heart into seeing more than there was again.

Penn had taken something from me.

Something I could never reclaim.

My innocence.

Oh, how cruel it was.

CHAPTER 13

SIX YEARS LATER

"*D*on't you just miss Charleston summers?" Amy asked.

We were sitting on beach chairs outside of her family's beachside home in Charleston. It was a roasting eighty-five degrees, and we were both lathered in sunscreen with big floppy hats on.

"Sometimes," I told her.

I'd spent this last summer in Aspen, Colorado, watching a vacation home for an uber wealthy woman from New York. She had wanted someone to take care of things for her in the off-season. I was finally starting to get used to living in these towns when no one was there. Paris in the fall, Turks and Caicos in the winter, Aspen for spring and summer.

"I don't know why you are taking these jobs, Nat. You know that you can do better than this."

I'd heard this routine time and time again.

"I did a year of working here and hated it, Amy. I

can't come back here and do that again. Plus, let's see… all expenses paid to travel destinations around the world with free lodging and unlimited time to write. Plus, I get paid. You do the math."

"You get paid enough to eat," Amy said. "If I'd known, when my parents offered you the opportunity to watch their place in Paris, that this would start an obsession, then I would have told them to hire it out in an Airbnb."

"You're such a great friend."

"Oh, I know." Amy turned to face me, pulling down her sunglasses. "So, how *is* the new manuscript coming along?"

I groaned. "Never ask a writer that. The answer is always horrible. It's horrible. The book sucks. It's never going to sell. My agent thinks I'm a hack, and basically, my life is over."

"So dramatic," Amy said with a laugh. "I doubt your agent thinks you're a hack. She signed off on your first manuscript, right?"

"Yeah. The one that didn't sell. And the one after that hasn't sold either."

"It's only been two years since graduation, Nat. You'll catch your break."

I shrugged. "Maybe."

"You could always self-publish them."

"I would. I really would if I wrote in a different genre. Do you remember Mindi from that Lit class I took?"

Amy nodded.

"She self-publishes and is making bank. Why did I decide to write literary fiction again?"

"Because you clearly hate yourself."

"Oh, right," I muttered with an eye roll.

"How long do I have you back in town anyway?" Amy asked.

"I don't know. Maybe your dream will come true, and I'll be here indefinitely." I tugged my hat lower. "I don't have a gig waiting for me. I've put out my resume and recommendations on my agency website that pairs vacation home watchers with vacation homes. I mentioned that I was looking for something else to Elizabeth when I left Aspen, but she is always up in space."

"Psh, you'll find something and be whisked away from me again."

"You can come stay for a weekend."

Amy grinned at me. "That is a perk of this weird job."

"I can't even believe that you think this is weird. You're the one who did a study abroad where you fucked your way through the Italian Renaissance."

"Priorities," Amy said with a hair flip. "And who are you fucking nowadays?"

My phone started ringing noisily from my beach bag. "Oh, look, saved by the bell."

"We're not done with this conversation."

"Oh, yes, we are," I said, grabbing my phone.

It wasn't a number I recognized, but I'd gotten used to that after working in this business. Being a vacation home watcher for the uber wealthy generally meant getting random phone calls at weird times of the day and meeting with strangers at the houses for upgrades during the off-season. It wasn't my favorite part of the job.

"Hello, this is Natalie."

"Natalie, this is Larkin St. Vincent. I work for Mayor Kensington's office."

I racked my brain for why this information was relevant. "The mayor of…"

"New York City," Lark said as if I were daft.

"Oh, wow! Okay. Well, so nice to speak with you. How can I help you?"

"You were recommended to Mayor Kensington by Elizabeth Cunningham as a vacation home watcher. She's looking for someone to watch her Hamptons home after Labor Day weekend."

My eyes bugged. Elizabeth had recommended me to the mayor of New York? Holy shit! Maybe she was even better connected than I'd thought.

"That sounds like a great opportunity," I managed to get out.

"Great. I'll send over the details and everything Mayor Kensington has in mind. Let me know if you have any questions. You can always reach me on this line."

"Thank you. I really appreciate it."

"Thank you, Natalie."

The line went dead, and I stared down at it in shock.

"What is it?" Amy asked.

"The mayor of New York City just asked me to watch her house in the Hamptons."

Amy jumped to her feet and screamed, "Oh my god! That's amazing!"

My hands were shaking as I dropped my phone into my beach bag. This was it. This was my break in this business. It might be strange, and I might not have been doing it for very long, but I was already in love with it.

And I couldn't wait to have several months on the beach in New York to finish off my latest manuscript in peace.

No parents.

No guys.

No distractions.

Just uninterrupted hours of writing.

It was almost too good to be true.

TO BE CONTINUED

Find out what happens with Penn & Natalie in *USA Today* bestselling author K.A. Linde's new billionaire romance…

CRUEL MONEY
(Cruel, #1)

She was supposed to be a one night stand. A way to sate my sexual appetite.

I let her glimpse the man I am. The face that I hide behind my carefully cultivated life. But she ripped open that divide—and there's no going back.

Now, she's here. In my city. I don't care that I'm Manhattan royalty and she's the help. Only that she's living in my summer home. With me.

And I want more.

Coming January 22nd! Preorder now!

Turn the page to start reading!

CHAPTER 1

CRUEL MONEY

Dear Natalie,

Here are the latest rejection letters from publishers regarding TOLD YOU SO. I will follow up with a list from Caroline of the remaining publishers who have the manuscript out on submission.

Regards,

Meredith Mayberry
    Assistant to Caroline Liebermann
    Whitten, Jones, & Liebermann Literary

Enclosed:

From Hartfield:

TOLD YOU SO has an interesting take on the value and cost of friendship. I enjoyed the journey the characters take and style of prose. But, unfortunately, that's where my praise ends. The heroine, Karla, was a caricature of bad judgment and a complete Mary Sue in every other regard. She's plain, ordinary, and not at all interesting enough to follow for 100k words. I felt Tina might have been a better lead, but it wasn't clear from the start whether the author was knowledgeable enough to convey the true depth of either of the characters. Perhaps the author should find a muse.

From Warren:

Natalie definitely knows how to tell a story and pull the reader in with a clever introduction. I just didn't find the characters relatable or the story high concept enough for what Warren is looking for right now. For us, we weren't completely sold on the genre, as it straddles the line between women's fiction and literary and thus, sits with neither.

From Strider:

TOLD YOU SO could have been great. Karla and Tina have so much potential, and the concept, while like several things we already have in our catalog, could have been brilliant. However, I never believed in their friendship, and the middle fell flat. The pace was slow, and for once, I was actually wishing there were a romance to break up the monotony. Maybe a more talented writer could have pulled this off.

"*F*uck," I groaned. "I get the message."

I threw my phone on the cushion next to me. No need to torture myself by reading any more of *that*. I couldn't even believe my agent would send me those comments. Let alone on a Friday night before she left for the weekend. Even worse that it came through from her assistant with all those horrible notes about my writing.

Was this the writing on the wall? My agent was finally finding out that I was a hack. Two books and two years later with no offers and pile after pile of heartbreaking rejections. Maybe this was the end.

I stared around the beautiful Hamptons beach house I was vacation home–watching this fall. I'd been hired a month ago and shown up only three days prior, determined to finish my next manuscript. It was a dream come true to be here without any distractions— no parents or guys or anything. Just me and my computer screen.

Then, my agent had gone and dropped the biggest distraction imaginable on my plate. I glared at my screen.

Oh, hell no.

Hell. No.

I was not letting these letters set me back. Maybe TOLD YOU SO wasn't *the* book, but the next one might be.

No, I needed to cleanse myself of this bullshit. I didn't normally subscribe to my mother's New Age spiritualism. She spent her spare time reading about auras, staring into crystal balls, and divining from the stars. It was a running joke in my life at this point. But there was a time and place for everything. And, if I was going to get something done during the next couple of months, I needed to leave the past behind me.

I knew what I was going to do.

I was going to burn this motherfucker to the ground.

Okay, maybe a little dramatic. Even for me.

But, hey, this was on the publishers. Was it so hard to craft a kind rejection email?

It's not you; it's me.

Maybe we can just be friends.

Come on. I'd heard it all from guys. Publishers could have the decency to try not to break my heart.

Ugh, fucking rejection.

But a plan had already formed, and I wasn't going to back down now.

I set my laptop up next to the printer in the office library with a bay window overlooking the ocean. I'd planned to write at that window nook. And I still wanted to. I pressed print on the computer and left to raid the stocked Kensington family wet bar. I'd have to replace whatever I scavenged, but it felt worth it tonight.

I was only watching the house through the fall season. I'd gotten the job after watching my best friend's parents' flat in Paris last summer. Word of mouth moved me around the world from there. From Paris to Turks and Caicos to Aspen, and now, I was watching the mayor of New York City's summer home in the Hamptons. And the mayor had a damn good selection of alcohol.

"Jefferson's Ocean: Aged at Sea," I muttered to myself.

Good enough for me. I grabbed the bottle and went in search of everything else I needed.

Fifteen minutes later, I had the stack of papers, a packet of matches, and the bottle of bourbon. I hoisted a shovel onto one shoulder on my way out the back door. When I hit the sand, I kicked off my shoes, grabbed a fistful of my flowy dress, and traipsed across the beach. My eyes were cast forward, and I moved with a sense of determination. The sun had finally left the horizon, throwing me into darkness, which was good, considering I was about to commit arson.

When I reached the soft sand right before the waterline, I dropped my supplies and dug my shovel into the sand. The first shovelful was incredibly satisfying. I took out my frustration and aggravation on that hole. Driving into the sand like I could erase the words from my brain. The tension in my shoulders intensified as I dug until I hit the wet sand beneath, and then I tossed my shovel to the side.

I reached for the supplies, and with my foot on the pages so that they didn't blow away, I unscrewed the top of the bottle of bourbon and took a large mouthful. The liquid burned its way down my throat. I sputtered and then took another.

That made me feel steadier. More alive. I shuddered as the alcohol hit me and then put it aside before retrieving the most important part of all of this.

Pages and pages and pages.

Forty-seven pages to be exact.

Forty-seven perfectly polite, perfectly soul-crushing pages.

Every rejection letter I'd ever gotten in the last two years, including the latest batch my agent had just sent over.

My eyes skimmed over the first page before I balled it up and threw it into the pit. A smile stretched on my face as I tossed page after page after page in the sand. Forty-seven pages of kindling.

I grinned wickedly, ready to put all of this rejection behind me.

I snatched up the bottle of bourbon and liberally poured it on the pages, like adding milk to cereal. Careful to move the bottle far enough away so that it wouldn't blow up in my face, I snatched up the box of matches.

"This is for you," I called up to the moon. "My ritual burning, my offering of this energy. Just take it away and help me start over."

I struck the match against the box and dropped it into the pit. When the first spark touched the fuel, the papers burst into flames, sending a jet of flames up toward the heavens. I laughed and danced in a circle around the flames, already feeling lighter.

So, maybe this book wasn't the one. Maybe this hadn't changed the world. But maybe the next one...or the next one. And, even if it was none of them, I was a writer. I would never stop writing.

A weight dropped off my shoulders, and I tilted my

head back toward the moon. I flung my hands out to the sides and did a poorly executed turn, tripped over my own feet, and landed in a heap in the sand. But nothing could stop the euphoria that settled in my chest. Who knew it would be so liberating to burn my rejection letters?

All I'd wanted was to change my luck and let the past go, but damn I felt like a million bucks.

The flames grew and grew, burning through the last two years of my life. And I rode the high as power threaded through me, leaving me drunk and not just from the bourbon.

Jumping back to my feet, I didn't even bother glancing down the beach. No one was in the Hamptons during the off-season. That was why I'd been hired to take care of the place during the interior renovation. Just last weekend, wealthy children of wealthy businessmen and wealthy politicians and wealthy celebrities had flocked to these beaches and overrun them at all hours of the day. But tonight, I was safe.

I wrenched at the bottom of my dress and lifted all the many layers of flowy material over my head. Tossing it into the sand, I unclasped my bra and discarded it as well. Then with a cry of triumph, I walked with my head held high straight into the ocean. The water was a bit frigid, and I shivered against the first wave that broke against my naked body. But I didn't care. I wasn't here for a swim. I was here for primal cleansing. Burn the negative energy and wash away the last remnants.

I dunked my head under the water and laughed

when I breached the surface. This was what it was to live. This was what I needed to remember. Life went on.

The Kensington house was just another job. Just another way to make a living while I pursued my passion. One day, I would catch a break, but until then, I would be damned if I let those publishers bring me down. I'd put one foot in front of the other and make it work.

Confident that the ritual burning and impromptu skinny-dipping had done its job, I hurried back out of the water. My steps were light as air, and my smile was magnetic. Whatever spell my mother's crazy life-journey had cast over all of this nonsense, it sure seemed to work. Believe in anything enough, and belief would turn into reality.

But as I was tramping back up to the fire to collect my clothes, I realized with horror that I wasn't alone. And what was worse, I recognized the man standing there.

I never forgot a face. And definitely not *that* face. Or the built body. Or the confident stance.

No, even though six years had passed, I would never forget Penn.

Or what he'd done to me.

CHAPTER 2

CRUEL MONEY

$\mathcal{M}$y dream and nightmare stood before me.

Clothed like a god walking off of a James Bond set with dark hair and midnight-blue eyes that flickered in the dying embers. Six years had only intensified his magnetic allure. The sharp planes of his too-beautiful face. The ever-present smirk, which sat prominent on those perfect lips. The coy glance as he slid his hands into the front pockets of his black suit pants.

I had been a girl then. Young, naive, and incredibly innocent. I'd thought him a man—bold, honest, emotive, and utterly larger than life. Now, as I looked upon him, I had no idea how I'd thought of him as anything but a rogue. The kind of man who could charm you with a glance and entice you out of your pants with a few pointed words. The sort of man I purposely walked away from now.

I'd never imagined I'd see him again. Never considered what would happen if I came face-to-face with him. But, now that I was, the words just tumbled from my mouth.

"What the fuck are you doing here?" I gasped.

He cocked his head to the side in surprise. An emotion I was sure that he wasn't accustomed to. He was definitely the kind of man who liked his life in a certain order. People didn't surprise him. He didn't let people in his life enough for that.

"What am *I* doing here?"

His voice was just as I remembered it. Smooth as butter and deeply entrancing. I thought I'd made it up. Like no one actually talked like this. In my mind, I'd magnified everything he was and everything he'd done. But standing here, I was wondering if I had remembered him better than I gave myself credit for.

I braced myself for this conversation. I'd built steel walls up around my heart, mind, and body. I didn't let people in as easily. And I needed to prepare myself for his manipulation. Let the anger I'd harbored all of these years tear him down as he had once hurt me.

"That's what I said," I snapped back.

I'd finally reached him, and I scrambled for my dress. It was a floor-length white boho number that had more fabric than sense, which made finding how to get it on *incredibly* difficult under good circumstances.

These were not good circumstances.

I struggled with the dress and the layers of material, desperate to find the opening for me to slip my head through. As if it wasn't bad enough that I was seeing

Penn again for the first time in six years, I had to do it completely naked.

Seemed fitting. That was the last way he'd seen me then, too.

"Yes, but you are the one who is out of place, skinny-dipping on this beach. Don't you know these are private residences?"

"I'm well aware."

I finally found the bottom to the dress and yanked it over my soaking wet head. My long silvery-white hair was such a nuisance sometimes. If only I'd let my best friend, Amy, convince me to chop off my ass-length hair, but no. I had to have another weapon to make getting my dress on more difficult.

"And you're only supposed to have bonfires in preapproved metal containers." He glanced down at my makeshift fire. It had almost completely died out by now. "Not to mention, have at least a two-gallon bucket of water to douse the flames."

I rolled my eyes. Was he actually serious right now?

My euphoria from the ritual began to evaporate. Well, that hadn't lasted long.

With a huff, I ruffled the bottom layers, pulled my sopping wet hair out of the back of the dress, and then grabbed the shovel off of the ground. With a mighty heave, I covered up the dying flames with a heap of sand.

"There!" I spat. "Now, can we get back to what is important? Like what you're doing here after all this time."

He frowned, as if confused by my statement. And that was when it hit me.

He didn't remember me.

Penn had no *clue* who the hell I was.

Oh god.

I hadn't thought that this could get worse or more humiliating. Sure, I looked like a crazy person, burning soul-crushing rejection letters and then stripping nude into the Atlantic. But, now the guy I'd cursed for *years* was standing before me … and he was staring at me as if I were a stranger.

Six years was a long time.

It was.

Most people might not remember someone that they'd had a one-night stand with from that long ago. I knew it was maybe a little irrational to be upset about it all. But, fuck it, I *was* upset.

You didn't have the most amazing night of your life with a total stranger and then completely forget that person! I didn't care who the hell you were. I didn't care how many times you'd had a one-night stand.

And it had been pretty clear that it wasn't Penn's first time—though it had been mine—but still, how could he have forgotten me?

"After all this time?" he asked.

"Never mind," I grumbled. "The real question is, what are you doing here? Do you live nearby? I thought this was the wrong time of year for the rich and entitled to be in the Hamptons. Memorial Day to Labor Day, right?"

I couldn't keep the snark out of my voice. No point

in filling the bastard in on how I knew him. If he lived nearby, this was going to be one hellacious house-watching.

"Most people are gone. But this is my home, which is why I was wondering what you were doing here."

"This is *your* home?" I whispered, pointing at the house off the beach. "No, this belongs to Mayor Kensington. She hired me to watch it this fall. You can't possibly own that house."

He shrugged and then sighed. "I didn't think anyone would be here," he said, clearly frustrated at my appearance.

"But…but…why would you…"

Then, it dawned on me. My heart stopped. My jaw dropped. I released a sharp breath in disbelief.

"You're a Kensington."

He gave me a sheepish grin. "I suppose it's my family home."

"You have *got* to be fucking kidding me." I shook my head in disbelief.

I thought this ritual was supposed to cleanse shit from my life. Not bring in another issue. Fuck.

I could not deal with this right now. Not with my anxiety high from the rejection letters. I'd only been here three days. I'd thought this was a dream come true. Everything was pointing me to get the fuck out of Dodge. Because, man, what *else* was life going to throw at me? Everything always came in threes. That was what my mom had said.

"I can't," I said. I held up my hand to keep him from saying anything. Then, I grabbed the remaining matches and the bourbon, which he eyed curiously, and then stomped off with the shovel over my shoulder.

"Um…where are you going?"

"I don't want to talk to you," I told him.

I didn't care that I was being incredibly unprofessional. Or that I was probably ruining my chance at staying at this house. Not that I wanted to work for the woman who had *birthed* this asshole. But I just needed to get away. I needed to get away and decompress and figure out how to proceed. If I saw his gorgeous face and that come-hither smile anymore, I was likely to stab him with the shovel.

Penn didn't seem to listen though. He barged right up the beach after me. Heedless of the sand in his loafers or messing up his probably bajillion-dollar suit.

"Uh, you left this," he said, holding out my bra.

I squeaked, juggled my full load, and snatched it out of his hand. Just fucking great. It wasn't the first time he'd held my bra or anything, but, god, at some point, I had to catch a break. I had to.

"You're welcome," he muttered under his breath.

I had no intention of thanking him for anything. So, I kept my mouth shut.

"Are you going to tell me why you seem like you're ready to set *me* on fire?" he asked. He was calm—curious but calm.

I was a puzzle he needed to solve. He needed to be able to put me in a box so that he could figure out how to manipulate my emotions to his whim.

"No."

"All right," he said. But it only made him inspect me harder. "I really don't understand why you're mad. This is my house. I thought you were the one trespassing."

"Well, I'm not," I growled. "I got this job a month ago. And I had *no* idea that you were going to be here. In fact, I had no idea you were even a Kensington."

He peered at me inquisitively, as if he were memorizing the span of my face and the curve of my figure. As if he were about to take a test and was having a last-minute cram session to remember all the little things he already knew about me but promptly forgot. "Have we met before?"

I snorted. "Observant."

"And it was a bad meeting?"

I snapped my narrowed eyes to him.

He held his hands up. "Okay. Very bad meeting."

"The fact that you don't even remember is…" I trailed off.

"Bad?"

"Reprehensible."

"You know, you do look familiar. I thought you did this whole time."

I rolled my eyes skyward and then deposited the shovel back where I'd found it. Better to keep it out of arm's reach for the rest of this conversation. "Don't bullshit me."

"I wasn't."

"Sure," I said sarcastically.

I wasn't sure he knew how to do anything else.

"No, really, how do I know you?"

I shook my head. Hurt broke through the anger.

Hurt that I hadn't let myself feel in so long. "If you can't remember, then I don't really see any reason to enlighten you."

Then, I reached for the door, but he stopped me in my tracks.

"Paris."

I whipped around in shock. He *did* remember. That bastard did remember something. But hurt was then immediately replaced with that boiling anger. That righteous, vindictive flame that shot through me every time I remembered my first time.

I yanked the door open and glared back at him. "That's right. We had one night in Paris. You wooed me, you fucked me, and then you ghosted!"

Pushing the door the rest of the way open, I stepped into the Kensington summer cottage. And I froze in place as four people turned to face me. Four people who had clearly heard me screaming at Penn and airing our dirty laundry.

Just...wonderful.

* * *

To continue reading, preorder **CRUEL MONEY** now.
Coming January 22nd!

ACKNOWLEDGMENTS

I spent five blissful days in Paris this summer. When I came home, I just knew that I had to write this book. I had to show Natalie and Penn's beginning and immerse myself in all the things that I absolutely adored about the city. It felt like coming home when I wrote it. I feel thankful every day that I get to bring stories to life in all of my favorite places.

Thank you to everyone who helped with this prequel. But especially Katie, Miller, and my husband, Joel, who traipsed all over Paris with me as I stared around with big doe-eyes at everything in sight.

If you want to read more about Penn & Natalie, grab Cruel Money coming January 22nd!

ABOUT THE AUTHOR

K.A. Linde is the *USA Today* bestselling author of the Avoiding Series, Wrights, and more than thirty other novels. She has a Masters degree in political science from the University of Georgia, was the head campaign worker for the 2012 presidential campaign at the University of North Carolina at Chapel Hill, and served as the head coach of the Duke University dance team. She loves reading fantasy novels, binge-watching Supernatural, traveling, and dancing in her spare time.

She currently lives in Lubbock, Texas, with her husband and two super-adorable puppies.

Visit her online at www.kalinde.com and on Facebook, Twitter, and Instagram @authorkalinde.

Join her newsletter at www.kalinde.com/subscribe for exclusive content, free books, and giveaways every month.